WHICHWOOD

WHICHWOOD

by
TAHEREH
MAFI

Dutton Children's Books

DUTTON CHILDREN'S BOOKS
Penguin Young Readers Group
An imprint of Penguin Random House LLC
375 Hudson Street
New York, NY 10014

Library of Congress Cataloging-in-Publication Data

Names: Mafi, Tahereh, author.
Title: Whichwood / by Tahereh Mafi.
Description: New York, NY : Dutton Children's Books Young Readers/Penguin
Random House LLC, [2017] | Companion to: Furthermore. | Summary: Laylee,
thirteen, is nearly worn out from washing and packaging corpses for the
Otherwhere and being shunned by villagers when two strangers, Alice and
Oliver, arrive determined to help.
Identifiers: LCCN 2017020411| ISBN 9781101994795 (hardcover) | ISBN
9781101994818 (ebook)
Subjects: | CYAC: Fantasy. | Magic—Fiction. | Dead—Fiction. | Friendship—Fiction.
Classification: LCC PZ7.M2695 Whi 2017 | DDC [Fic]—dc23 LC record available at
https://lccn.loc.gov/2017020411

Printed in the United States of America

1   3   5   7   9   10   8   6   4   2

Edited by Julie Strauss-Gabel

Text set in ITC Esprit Std

For my parents,
for the long nights spent reading Persian poetry
over endless cups of tea

OUR STORY
BEGINS ON A
FROSTY NIGHT

Infant snow drifted down in gentle whorls,
flakes as large as pancakes glinting silver as they fell. Shaggy
trees wore white leaves and moonlight glimmered across a
glassy lake. The night was soft and all was slow and snow had
hushed the earth into a deep, sound slumber and oh, winter
was fast approaching.

For the town of Whichwood, winter was a welcome distraction; they thrived in the cold and delighted in the ice (the very
first snowfall was terribly nice), and they were well equipped
with food and festivities to keep toasty throughout the season.
Yalda, the biggest celebration, was the winter solstice, and the
land of Whichwood was electric with anticipation. Whichwood was a distinctly magical village, and Yalda—the town's
most important holiday—was a very densely magical evening.
Yalda was the last night of fall and the longest night of the
year; it was a time of gift-giving and tea-drinking and endless
feasting—and it was a great deal more than that, too. We're a
bit pressed for minutes at the moment (something strange is

soon to happen and I can't be distracted when it does), so we'll discuss the finer details at a later time. For now, know this: Every new snowfall arrived with a foot of fresh excitement, and with only two days left till winter, the people of Whichwood could scarcely contain their joy.

With a single notable exception.

There was only one person in Whichwood who never partook in the town merriment. Only one person who drew closed her curtains and cursed the song and dance of a magical evening. And she was a very strange person indeed.

Laylee hated the cold.

At thirteen years old, she'd long lost that precious, relentless optimism reserved almost exclusively for young people. She'd no sense of whimsy, no interest in decadence, no tolerance for niceties. No, Laylee hated the frost and she hated the fuss and she resented not only this holiday season, but even those who loved it. (To be fair, Laylee resented many things—not the least of which was her lot in life—but winter was the thing she resented perhaps most of all.)

Come sleet or snow, she alone was forced to work long hours in the cold, her kneecaps icing over as she dragged dead bodies into a large porcelain tub in her backyard. She'd scrub limp necks and broken legs and dirty fingernails until her own fingers froze solid, and then she'd hang those dead, dragging limbs up to dry—only to later return and break icicles off corpse chins and noses. Laylee had no holidays, no vacations, not even a set schedule. She worked when her customers came calling, which meant very soon she'd be worked to the bone. Winter in Whichwood, you see, was a very popular season for dying.

Tonight, Laylee was found frowning (her expression of choice), irritated (perhaps more than usual), bundled (to the point of asphyxiation), and stubbornly determined to catch a few snowflakes before dinner. Fresh flakes were the thickest and the crispest, and a rare treat if you were quick enough to catch a few.

If I may: I know it seems a strange idea, eating snowflakes for dinner, but you have to understand—Laylee Layla Fenjoon was a very strange girl, and despite (or perhaps because of) the oddness of her occupation, she was in desperate need of a treat. She'd had to wash nine very large, thoroughly rotted persons today—this was four more than usual—and it had been very hard on her. Indeed, she often caught herself dreaming of a life where her family didn't run a laundering business for the deceased.

Well, I say *family,* but it was really just Laylee doing all the washing. Maman had died two years prior (a cockroach had fallen in the samovar and Maman, unwittingly, drank the tea; it was all very tragic), but Laylee was not afforded the opportunity to grieve. Most ghosts moved on after a good scrubbing, you see, but Maman's had lingered, floating about the halls and criticizing Laylee's best work even when she was sleeping. Baba, too, was entirely absent, as he'd been gone just as long

5

as Maman had been dead. Devastated by the loss of his wife, he'd set off on an impulsive journey not two days after Maman died, determined to find Death and give him a firm talking-to about his recent choices.

Sadly, Death was nowhere to be found.

Worse, grief had so thoroughly crippled Baba's mind that, despite his two-year absence, thus far he'd managed to travel only as far as the city center. In his heartbreak he'd lost not only his way, but his good sense, too. Baba's brain had rearranged, and in the madness and chaos of loss, no room remained for his only child. Laylee was collateral damage in a war on grief, and Baba, who had no hope of winning such a war, haplessly succumbed to this opiate of oblivion. Laylee would often pass her disoriented father on her sojourns into town, pat his shoulder in a show of support, and tuck a pomegranate into his pocket.

More on that later.

For now, let us focus: It was a cold, lonely night, and Laylee had just collected the last of her dinner when a sudden sound froze her still. Two loud thumps, a branch snap, a dull thud, the unmistakable intake of air and a sudden rush of angry whispers—

No, there was no denying it: There were trespassers here.

Now, this would have been an alarming revelation for any normal person, but as Laylee was a distinctly abnormal person, she remained unperturbed. She was, however, perplexed.

The thing was, no persons *ever* came here, and heaven help them if they did; stumbling upon a shed of swollen, rotting corpses had never done any person any good. It was for this reason that Laylee and her family lived in relative isolation. They had taken up residence in a small, drafty castle on a little peninsula on the outer edge of town in an informal sort of exile; it was an unkindness Laylee and her family had not earned, but then, no one wanted to live next door to the girl with such an unfortunate occupation.

In any case, Laylee was entirely unaccustomed to hearing human voices so close to home, and it made her suspicious. Her head high and alert, Laylee stacked her snowflakes into an ornate silver dinnerbox—an old family heirloom—and tiptoed out of sight.

Laylee wasn't a child oft bothered by the fuss and furor of fear; no, she dealt with death every day, and so the unknowns that startled most had little effect on a person who could talk to ghosts. (This last bit was a secret, of course—Laylee knew better than to tell her townspeople that she could see and speak with the spirits of their loved ones; she had no interest in being asked to do more work than was already stacked in her shed.) So as she trod cautiously back toward the modest castle that was her home, she felt not fear, but a tickle of curiosity, and as the feeling warmed itself inside her heart, she blinked, grateful and surprised to feel a smile spreading across her face.

Maman was hovering in the entryway as Laylee pulled open the heavy wooden door and, just as the ghost-mother prepared to shout about one new grievance or another, a sudden gust of wind slammed shut the door behind them, causing Laylee to jolt against her will. She closed her eyes and exhaled sharply, her hands still closed around her silver box.

"Where have you been?" Maman demanded, zipping around Laylee's ears. "Don't you care at all about my feelings? You know how lonely I get, locked up here all by myself—"

(Right, yes, this was another thing: Maman would haunt their home and nowhere else—not because she *couldn't*, but because she wouldn't. She was a very doting parent.)

Laylee ignored Maman. Presently, she untied an ancient, floral, excessively fringed scarf from around her head and unbuttoned the toggles of her fur-lined winter cloak, hanging both to dry by the front door. The fur was a gift from a fox who'd saved his summer sheddings for her, and tonight Laylee had been especially grateful for the extra warmth.

"—no one to talk to," Maman was wailing, "no one to sympathize with my plight—"

Laylee used to be more sympathetic to Maman's plights, but she'd learned the hard way that this ghost was but an echo of her real mother. Maman had been a vibrant, interesting woman, but the gauzy iteration flitting past our heroine's head had little personality and even less charm. Ghosts, it turned out, were excessively insecure creatures, offended by every imagined slight; they required constant coddling and found comfort only in their romantic musings on death—which, as you might imagine, made them miserable companions.

Maman had settled into a dramatic soliloquy—taking care to describe the monotony of her day in great detail—as Laylee took a seat at the kitchen table. She didn't bother lighting a lamp, as there weren't any lamps to be lit. She'd been on her own for two years now, fending for herself and footing the bills, but no matter how hard Laylee worked, it was never enough to bring her home back to life. Laylee had one gift: She had a magical talent that enabled her (and those of her bloodline—she'd inherited the gene from Baba) to wash and package the dead destined for the Otherwhere, but such heavy work was never meant to be carried out by a single person—and certainly not by one so young. Despite her best efforts, Laylee's body was slowly deteriorating; and the longer her small person dealt in the decomposition of life, the weaker she became.

Laylee didn't have the time to be a vain girl, but if she'd ever spent more than a few minutes in front of a mirror she might have blossomed into a fine narcissist. In fact, had her parents been around to encourage her ego, she might well have lost the whole of her mind. It was lucky for Laylee, then, that she had neither mother nor mirror to fill her head with nonsense, for a closer inspection of her reflected self would have revealed a girl of unusual beauty. She was of slim, sturdy build, with long, elegant limbs; but it was her eyes—soft and doll-like— that set her apart. One look at our young friend was enough to flutter the hearts of those who met her, but it was that second glance that awakened their fear. Let us be clear: Laylee's looks did not inspire admirers. She was not a girl to be trifled with, and her beauty was to her as inconsequential as those who revered it. She was born beautiful, you see; her face was a gift she could not shed.

At least, not yet.

The work she did was taking its toll, and she could no longer ignore the changes in her reflection. Though her chestnut locks had once been lustrous and robust, they'd now begun to fade: Laylee was going silver from the ends upward, and her eyes—which had once been a deep, rich amber—had gone a glassy gray. Thus far, only her skin had been spared; even so, her newly flinty eyes against the deep bronze of her skin made her seem moon-like, alien, and perpetually sad. But Laylee had little patience for sadness, and though deep down she felt a great deal of pain, she much preferred to be angry.

And so she was, for the most part, an irritable, unkind, angry girl, with little pleasantness to distract her from the constant death demanding her attention. Tonight, she swept a defeated glance around the many rooms of her drafty home and promised herself that one day she would do well enough to repair the broken windows, mend the torn draperies, replace the missing torches, and reinvigorate the faded walls.

Though she worked hard every day, Laylee was seldom paid for the work she did. The magic that ran through her veins made it so she was bound by blood to be a *mordeshoor,* and when the dead were delivered to her door, she had no choice but to add them to the pile. The people of Whichwood knew this and too often took advantage of her, sometimes paying very little, and sometimes not at all. But one day, she swore, she'd breathe light and color back into the dimness that had diminished her life.

Maman was darting in and out of her daughter's face again, unhappy to be so soundly ignored. Laylee swatted at Maman's insubstantial figure, her face pulled together in dismay. The daughter ducked twice and eventually gave up, carrying her dinner into the sparsely furnished living room and, once newly settled onto the softest part of the threadbare rug, Laylee cracked open the dinnerbox. The room was lit only by moonlight, but the distant orb would have to do. Laylee dropped her chin in one hand, crunched quietly on a snowflake the size of her face, and thought wistfully of the days she used to spend with children her own age. It had been a long time since Laylee had been to school, and she missed it sometimes. But school was a thing of luxury; it was meant for children with working parents and domestic stability—and Laylee could no longer pretend to have either.

She bit into another snowflake.

The first fresh flakes of the season were made entirely of sugar—this was a magic specific to Whichwood—and though Laylee knew she should eat something healthier, she simply didn't care. Tonight she wanted to relax. So she ate all five flakes in one sitting and felt very, very good about it.

Maman, meanwhile, had just concluded her monologue and was now moving on to more pressing issues (the general state of the house, the more specific mess in the kitchen, the dusty hallways, her daughter's damaged hair and callused hands) when Laylee retreated upstairs. This was Maman's daily routine, and Laylee was struggling to be patient about it. She'd stopped responding to Maman long ago—which helped a bit—but it also meant that sometimes several days would pass before Laylee would speak a single word, and the loneliness was beginning to scar. Laylee hadn't always been such a silent child, but the more anger and resentment welled up inside of her, the less she dared to say.

She was a girl who rarely spoke for fear of spontaneously combusting.

Laylee had locked herself in the toilet for far
longer than was necessary. The bathroom was the one place
Maman would not haunt her (just because she was dead did
not mean she'd lost her sense of decency), and Laylee cherished her time in this unholy space. She'd just finished mixing
a soaking solution in a copper basin (warm water, sugarsalt,
rosehip oil, and a snip of lavender) for her aching hands when
she noticed something strange.

It was slight, but it was there: The tips of her fingers were
going silver.

Laylee gasped so deeply she nearly knocked over the bowl.
She fell to her knees, rubbing at her skin like she might undo
the harm, but it was no use.

It had been hard enough to watch her eyes turn, and even
more devastating when her hair went, too, but this—this was
dire indeed. Laylee could not have known then the full ex-
tent of the damage she'd inflicted upon her body, but she knew

enough to understand this: She was irrevocably ill from the inside out, and she didn't know what to do.

Her first thought was to appeal to Baba.

She'd begged him countless times to return home, but he could never see the sense in her words. Baba had become increasingly delusional over the years, never certain whether he existed in the world of the living or the dead. After Maman died, he fully unzipped from what little sense he had left; now he was forever lost in transit, and there was nothing Laylee could do about it. *Just a little longer,* he'd always say, in his charming, clumsy way. *I'm nearly there.* Baba kept his teeth in his pocket, you see, so it was very difficult for him to enunciate.

I should explain.

Once upon a time, Baba had seen Maman at the marketplace and had very swiftly fallen in love with her. This wasn't an unusual occurrence for Maman; in fact, strangers had been known to fall in love with her with some frequency. She was, as you might have suspected, a supremely beautiful woman— but not in any common, familiar sort of way. No, Maman was the kind of beautiful that ruined lives and relieved men of their sanity. She had a face that was impossible to describe and skin so luminous it looked as though the sun itself had haunted her. And while it was true that many residents of Whichwood had beautiful skin (they were a golden kind of people, even in the winter, with brown skin bronzed by daylight), Maman outshone the lot of them, wrapping her hair in vibrant, fluid silks that made her glimmering skin appear absolutely *other*. And her eyes—deep and dazzling—were so captivating that passersby would faint dead away at the sight of her. (You might now hazard a guess as to how Laylee inherited her good looks.) Maman was courted by nearly every person brave enough to fight for her affection, and though she did not hate her beauty, she hated being defined by it, so she dismissed every suitor just as quickly as they came.

But Baba was different.

He wasn't particularly handsome, but he was a man who lived to get lost in emotion, and he was desperate to be in love. After learning that Maman worked at her family's dental practice, he made a plan. Every day—for just over a month—he paid to have a tooth pulled just to be able to spend time with her. He'd lie back and listen to her talk while she extracted healthy teeth from his open mouth, and each day he would stumble home bloody and aching and thoroughly, hopelessly in love. It was only after he'd run out of teeth that Maman finally fell for him, and though Baba was proud of their unusual courtship, Laylee found their story to be inexpressibly stupid, and it took no small amount of coaxing to convince her to share this memory.

I hope you are pleased.

In any case, Baba seemed a hopeless case. Laylee loathed and adored Baba with a great urgency, and though she thought fondly of their early years together, she also blamed him for being so recently careless. He was a man who felt too much, and his heart was so large that things got lost in it. Laylee knew she was an important part of him, but with so much in this world competing for his attention, the space she took up was disappointingly small.

And so it was there—cold and curled up on the toilet floor, clutching silvered fingers and pressing her lips together to keep from crying—that Laylee heard the unmistakable sound of glass shattering.

❖

Laylee flew out the bathroom door and into the hall. Her eyes darted around in search of damage, and for the first time in a long while, she felt the tiniest prickle of fear. It wasn't an unpleasant feeling.

Curiously, Maman's ghost was nowhere to be found. Laylee peered over the banister to the floor below, squinting to see where Maman might've gone, but the house was still. Alarmingly so.

And then: whispers.

Laylee snapped to attention and sharpened her ears, listening closely for any signs of danger. The whispers were rushed and rough—angry?—and it was only a moment longer before she realized the sounds were coming from her own bedroom. Her heart was beating faster now; fear and anticipation had collided within her and she was heady with an unusual kind of excitement. Nothing so mysterious had ever happened to her before, and she was surprised to find how much she liked it.

Laylee tiptoed toward her bedroom with graceful stealth, but when she pushed open the door to her room, eager to apprehend the intruder, Laylee was so startled by what she saw that she screamed, scrambled backward, and stubbed her toe so badly she screamed twice more.

"Please—don't be frightened—"

But Laylee was horrified. She fell back against the banister and tried to steady the rise and fall of her chest, but she was so untethered by the rush of these many rusty emotions that she couldn't gather the words to respond. Laylee had been expecting a renegade corpse, a rampaging ghost, perhaps a disturbed flock of geese—but no—most unexpected—

There was a *boy* in her room.

He was a pathetic-looking creature, half frozen, quickly melting, and generally drenched from head to toe. Worse: He was dripping dirty water all over her floor. Laylee was still too stunned to speak. He'd followed her into the hall, hands up, pleading with his eyes, and yet—he also appeared to be studying her. It was only when Laylee realized he was looking curiously at her hair that she reunited with her senses and ran downstairs.

Laylee snatched a poker from the fireplace before grabbing for her fringed scarf, throwing it over her head and securing it tightly around her neck. Her hands were shaking—shaking! so strange!—and she'd only just begun to brace herself for a fight when she heard the voice of someone new.

She spun around, breathing hard.

This time, it was a girl who stood facing her—also sopping wet—and it was the most peculiar-looking girl Laylee had ever seen. More confounding: The girl was not only shivering and clutching at her wet arms, she also appeared to be on the verge of tears.

"I'm so desperately sorry Oliver is an idiot," said the girl all at once, "but please don't be frightened. We're not here to harm you, I swear it."

Of this harmlessness, Laylee was beginning to feel certain.

The girl who stood before her was pocket-sized; she looked too delicate to be real. In fact, if Laylee hadn't already been acquainted with so many ghosts, she might've confused this stranger for a spirit. Her skin was a shocking shade of white, the same white as her hair, her eyebrows, and the flutter of thick, snow-bright lashes that framed her light brown irises— these, her only feature that held any color. She was an odd-looking person for the land of Whichwood, where the people were renowned for their golden-brown skin and rich, jewel-toned eyes. Laylee couldn't help but be curious about this unusual girl.

Her panic slowly subsiding, Laylee slackened her grip

around the poker. More than curious—there was something kind about this stranger, and though Laylee did not think of *herself* as a kind person, she was still rather fond of kindness itself. In any case, she was intrigued; it had been a very long time since she'd met another girl her own age.

"Who are you?" Laylee finally said, her voice rough from a lack of use.

"My name is Alice," said the girl, and smiled.

Laylee felt a tug at her heart; old habits encouraged her to smile back, but Laylee refused, choosing to frown instead. She cleared the cobwebs from her throat and said, "And why have you broken into my home?"

Alice looked away, embarrassed. "Oliver was the one who broke the window. I'm so sorry about that. I told him we should knock—that we should come inside the normal way— but we were so desperately cold that he insisted we go a more direct route and—"

"Oliver is the boy?"

Alice nodded.

"Where has he gone?" Laylee looked over Alice's head, searching for a glimpse of him.

"He's hiding," said Alice. "I think he's afraid you're going to kill him."

Laylee stopped searching and instead raised an eyebrow. She felt her lips twitch and again quashed the urge to smile.

"Might we please stay awhile?" said Alice timidly. "It's been a very long journey and we're dreadfully tired. It took forever to find you, you know."

Laylee clenched her fist around the poker again. "Find me?" she said. "Why did you want to find me?"

Alice blinked. "Well, we came to help you, of course."

"I don't understand," said Laylee. "How do you intend to help me?"

"Well, I'm"—Alice hesitated—"actually, I'm not really sure," she said, twisting her wet hair in her fingers. A small puddle was forming at her feet. "It's rather a long story. In fact—in fact I should probably tell you that we're not from here. We come from another village, called Ferenwood. You've probably never heard of Ferenwood, but it's ano—"

"Of course I know of Ferenwood," Laylee snapped. She hadn't had as much schooling as most children, but she wasn't stupid. "We study the many magical lands in our second year."

Alice's face went impossibly paler. "There are other magical lands? But I've only just learned about *you*."

Laylee was unmoved. This girl was either very stupid or just pretending to be stupid, and Laylee couldn't decide which was worse.

"Well, anyway," Alice rushed on, wringing her hands, "we have a Surrender every year where we perform our magical talents in exchange for a task, and—and anyhow, I've been tasked to you."

This, Laylee did not understand.

It took several minutes of explaining what, exactly, went into a *Surrender* (this was a magical coming-of-age ceremony specific to Ferenwood) and the mechanics of a task (the purpose of which was always to help someone or someplace in need), and by the end of it, Laylee was not only irritated, she was annoyed, and she wanted Alice to go home.

"I will not accept your pity," said Laylee. "You're wasting your time."

"But—"

"Take your friend and leave me be. I've had a very long day and I've more to do in the morning and I cannot be distracted by your"—she frowned and waved a dismissive hand—"bizarre offer of charity."

"No—please," Alice said quickly, "you must understand: I wouldn't have been sent here if you didn't have a problem I could fix! If you would only tell me what's wrong with you, maybe I could—"

"What's *wrong* with me?" said Laylee, astounded.

"Well, I don't mean"—Alice laughed nervously—"of course I didn't mean that there was anything *wrong* with you—"

"Good grief, Alice. Ruined things already, have you?" Oliver had appeared at her side with such silent swiftness he startled both girls at once.

"What are you doing here?" Laylee said angrily, turning to aim the poker in his direction. "Who *are* you people?"

"We're here to fix what ails you, apparently," said Oliver with a smile. "Alice is very smooth, isn't she? Quite the charmer."

Laylee, confused, dropped the poker for just a second. "What on earth are you talking about?"

"Ah," said Oliver, raising an eyebrow. "I see we've already lost our sense of humor."

"Oliver, *please*!" Alice cried. "Just be quiet!"

Laylee, who'd had quite enough of this nonsense, narrowed her eyes and clenched the poker and the next thing she knew she was making up beds for her guests and asking them if they'd like anything to drink. A great fire was blazing on the hearth, and the castle felt warm and cozy like it hadn't in years. Laylee was always loath to light a fire (as it was a costly indulgence), and she'd spent all year carefully amassing a steady supply of firewood; the most frigid winter nights were yet to come, and she was planning to ration what she had to last the snowy season. Now she smiled at the dancing flames, only partly understanding that these strangers had used up her entire store in a single evening, and she sighed, wondering—with great tenderness—how best to kill them for it.

✤

Alice and Oliver were now nice and dry. Their heavy coats had been hung by the fire and, thanks to the great and crackling blaze, were nearly rid of any remaining damp. Oliver seemed pleased. Alice, however, was looking newly terrified, shooting worried glances at Laylee (who was studying her hands, trying to determine left from right), tugging at her companion's shirt, and hissing, "Stop this, Oliver! You stop it right now!"

Laylee blinked.

"She's perfectly fine, Alice! There's no need for hysterics."

"If you don't stop this *right now*—"

"But she won't let us stay any other way! Besides, she'd have stuck you nice and bloody with that poker if it weren't for me—"

Laylee tilted her head, distracted by a spot on the wall. Dimly, she wondered who these people were.

"This is *my* task, Oliver Newbanks, and you will do as I say. And it's no fault of mine that she wanted to stick me with a poker! Maybe if you hadn't decided to break her bedroom window—"

"It was freezing outside!"

"Oh, I swear it, Oliver, if you ruin this for me, I will never forgive you, not ever!"

"Alright," he said with a sigh. "Fine. But I'm only doing it bec—"

Laylee inhaled so quickly she felt her head spin. Slowly, very slowly, she felt the blood rush back into her brain. She rubbed at her eyes and squinted them open, blinking carefully in the intense glow of the fire, but no matter how hard she tried, she couldn't make sense of what she saw. She couldn't remember how she'd gotten here, and she couldn't understand who'd allowed these strangers to set up quarters in her living room.

And then all at once, her senses returned.

She spun around, searching for her makeshift weapon, when Oliver cried, "Laylee—please!"

And she slowed.

She was almost afraid to ask how he knew her name.

He was holding up his hands in mock surrender, and Laylee felt she could hold off trying to kill this boy for at least long enough to get a good look at him.

His hair was silver like hers, but in a way that seemed natural. And his eyes—a shade of blue so rich they were nearly violet—were striking against his brown skin. Everything about him was sharp and polished (and handsome) and the longer she looked at him, the more she felt a sudden, fluttering thrill in her heart, and she was so unsettled by the sensation she nearly hit him with the poker just to be rid of it.

"We're not here to hurt you," he said. "Please—"

"You can't stay here." Laylee cut him off, nervous anger flaming her cheeks. "You're not allowed to be here."

"I know—I know it's not ideal to host a pair of guests you've never met, but if we could just explain—"

"No," Laylee said heavily, struggling to stay calm, "you don't understand. This home is protected by ancient magic. Only a mordeshoor may find refuge here."

Neither Alice nor Oliver appeared to be bothered by this revelation. Oliver, for his part, was still staring at Laylee, transfixed. "What's a *mordeshoor*?"

"It's what I am. It's the name given to those of us who wash the dead and package their bodies for the Otherwhere. We are mordeshoors."

"Goodness, that seems just awful," said Alice, patting Laylee's arm and looking overly sympathetic. Laylee bristled, snatching her arm away at once, but Alice didn't seem to notice; instead, she gestured to a chair. "Would you mind if I sat down?"

"You must leave," said Laylee sharply. *"Now."*

"Don't you worry about us," Oliver said with a smile. "We'll be fine—we're not afraid of a few dead people. We just need a warm place to rest awhile."

Laylee rolled her eyes so hard she nearly snapped a nerve. "You will not be *fine,* you fool. You have no protection here. You won't survive the night."

Alice finally showed a flicker of fear. "Why not?" she asked quietly. "What would happen?"

Laylee dragged her eyes over to Alice. "The ghosts of the freshly dead are always terrified to cross over—they'd much rather cling to the human life they know. But a spirit can only exist in the human world when it's wearing human skin." She leveled them both with a dark look. "If you stay here, they will harvest your flesh. They will make suits of your skin as you sleep and leave you rotting in your own blood."

Alice clapped both hands over her mouth.

"This is precisely why I exist," said Laylee. "The process of washing the body calms the wandering spirit; when the body crosses over, so too will the ghost."

(Maman, you will note, was an exception to this rule; I promise to explain the particulars at a quieter time.)

Alice pinched Oliver in the shoulder. "Do you see now?" She pinched him again. "Do you see what you nearly did? You nearly killed us with your cheating! Skin suits, indeed!"

Oliver frowned, flinched, and jumped away from Alice, rubbing his shoulder as he did. He was irritated, but somehow, simultaneously, fascinated.

"Now get out of my house." Laylee picked up the poker and jabbed them both, briefly, in the centers of their chests. "Out! Get out!"

Alice was crestfallen, but Laylee felt no remorse. These trespassers were not only flagrantly disrespecting her wishes, but they'd used up all her firewood, too, and Laylee couldn't take much more of their foolishness. This was *her* home—she alone should be able to choose who entered it.

She was parading the two of them toward the exit when Oliver said, "Let's say for a moment that you *did* want us to stay here—"

Laylee jabbed him in the back.

"In theory!" he said, wincing. "Let's just say, in theory, that you actually wanted us to stay here. Would we have to wash a dead body in order for the magic to protect us?"

Laylee shook her head.

Oliver was visibly relieved.

"Not just one," she said. "You'd have to wash three. A man, a woman, and a child; three for every night you remain."

Oliver blanched. "Do you even *have* that many dead people here?"

Laylee stopped walking. Quietly, she said, "Yes."

It was a single word, but it carried a great deal of weight. They three were suddenly overtaken by a silence within which each of them was, for a moment, tossed about in a tornado of their own worries. Laylee, weary with exhaustion, could think of little but her own steady deterioration; Oliver, wary of the situation, could focus on little but self-preservation; but Alice, who often took the time to worry about more than just herself, felt a door in her heart swing open.

It was she who finally said, with great tenderness, "That sounds like an awful lot of work for one person."

Laylee looked up sharply, locking eyes with Alice in a rare moment of transparency. The reminder of her workload had dropped a new weight on Laylee's shoulders; she felt her elbows unlock. She'd nearly forgotten the newly silver tips of her fingers until she'd felt them tremble, and it was enough to loosen her grip on the poker. She looked away as she said, "Yes. It is."

Alice shot Oliver a knowing look, and he seemed to understand. This was their moment. Together they stood tall, screwed up their courage, and said, "Well—would you like some help?"

And it was this—this simple, foolish question—that finally touched the heart of our young protagonist.

Something like hope had whistled through the cracks in her heart, surprising her with a feeling she'd long forgot. It was then that Laylee looked at her trespassers with new eyes. It was then, dear friends, that she finally smiled.

❖

Oh, it would be a very, very long night.

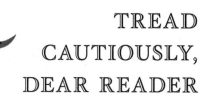

TREAD
CAUTIOUSLY,
DEAR READER

The moon hung fat and low in the half-lit sky as they three traipsed single-file into the backyard, Laylee leading the way. Night had fallen fast: a skin of darkness had been hitched across the daylight and left to rot until midnight itself had become a curtain of charred flesh you could pinch between two fingers. The clouds were stretched thin as they slunk by, gauzy strokes painted hither and thither. There were many dead lying about these grounds—and many ghosts haunting the hollows in between—but the real monster they faced tonight was the wintertide itself: The cold was a physical enemy, a blistering, forbidding presence stacked thickly in the air. Each step forward was an instigation of aggression, arms punching and heads knocking against icy gusts and fits. Laylee, at least, was well prepared for the wars waged by these freezing nights.

Her work was always done in uniform—in accordance with proper mordeshoor tradition—and she was never more grateful for the ancient armor of her ancestors than she was on these nights. She'd latched an old, intricately hammered chest plate atop her heavy, tattered gown, clamped solid gold cuffs on both forearms and ankles, and upon her head—secured atop her floral scarf—she wore the most impressive heirloom of all: an ancient helmet she wore only in the winters for its added protection against the blustery nights. It was a gold dome of a cap embellished with a series of ornate, hand-hammered flourishes; emblazoned all around the dome in timeworn calligraphy were wise words captured long ago, in a language she still loved to speak. It was the work of the poet Rumi, who'd written,

دی شیخ با چراغ همی‌گشت گرد شهر
کز دیو و دد ملولم و انسانم آرزوست

Last night a sheikh went all about the city, lamp in hand,
crying, "I'm weary of all these beasts and devils,
and desperately seek out humanity!"

The helmet was topped by a single proud spike that stood five inches tall; the brim adorned by hundreds of fussy hinges from which hung a fringe of jagged chainmail. The sheets of deftly braided steel rained down the back and sides of Laylee's head, swishing quietly as she walked, leaving dents in the wind. She was thirteen years old and far too terrifying for her age, but she was, at least, entirely prepared to deal with death on even these, the coldest nights of the year. Laylee tugged her scarf across her nose and mouth in a practiced motion, careful lest she breathe in too deeply (on more than one occasion she'd had to rush home for a glass of warm water, frost choking the inside of her throat), and soldiered on.

It was odd: Whichwood was known for its spectacularly painful winters, but this night seemed unusually cold. Laylee, as I mentioned, was armed and bundled to the point of immobility, but her companions were a sight less prepared. They'd at least known to travel with heavy winter cloaks and boots, but they were strangers to this land—their bones were not built to carry this cold—and more than once, Laylee caught herself wondering how they managed. She was sure these two had no idea what they'd agreed to, and part of her worried they'd be scared away too soon. It was only then that she saw how quickly she'd come to rely upon their offer of help, and she hated herself for it. Laylee was too proud to accept charity, but she was too smart to reject it, too. No one had ever before offered to help her, and she couldn't say no to a good thing now. Certainly *she* could stand to live with these children in exchange for their assistance—but would her fragile guests survive the night?

She dug the silver tips of her fingers into her palms and

clenched her jaw in frustration. Oh, if only she *could,* she'd rather die than accept the pity of passing strangers.

❖

The farther they walked, the deeper they dipped, and soon the triplet troop was caught thigh-high in the snow, and there was no telling how long they'd last. Laylee glanced briefly in her guests' direction, but thus far they'd not made a peep of protest, and Laylee couldn't help but feel a begrudging respect for their resilience. And so, for the first time in a long while, Laylee was inspired to do something kind.

She stopped abruptly, Alice and Oliver quickly following suit. It had been at least two years since Laylee had felt any compulsion to *share,* but tonight she was feeling more unusual than usual, so she unearthed a small pouch of matches from somewhere inside her cloak and offered its contents to her guests.

They didn't seem to understand.

Alice shook her head. "N-no, thank you," she stammered, cold caught in her teeth.

Oliver shook his head, too. "What's it for?"

"To keep you warm," said Laylee, confused and—dare I say it?—hurt.

"One m-match?" said Alice, still shivering. "Doesn't s-seem like it'd d-do much good."

Laylee withdrew her hand, stung by their rejection, and

looked away. She was ashamed of herself for having offered them anything at all. Angrily, she snatched a matchstick from the pouch and popped it in her mouth, vowing to never offer these ingrates anything again.

Alice gasped. "What are y—"

But Laylee's face had just flushed a bright red, and Alice couldn't be bothered to finish her sentence. The heat was moving quickly through Laylee's body, and her cheeks were now a sweet, rosy pink. The warmth would last only a short while, but it always helped her get through the rougher hours of winter workdays.

It was an awed Oliver who finally whispered, "What did you just do? I could've sworn you just ate a matchstick."

Laylee was feeling very warm and, suddenly, a little sleepy. She blinked softly and smiled, only vaguely aware that she'd done so. "Yes," she said. "I did."

"But—"

"I know," Laylee said quietly. "Some people don't approve of Quicks, but I can't say I care."

"It's not that at all," said Oliver. "We've just never seen such a thing before. We don't eat matches in Ferenwood."

Laylee looked up, slightly mollified. "Oh."

"How do they w-work?" said Alice, who was now standing in snow up to her waist.

"Well," said Laylee, as she tilted her head, "they don't work for everyone. But the idea is that they catch fire inside of you, heating you up from the inside out."

"That's f-fascinating," said Alice, who was now eyeing Laylee's pockets with a new hunger.

"Wait," said Oliver, "why don't they work for everyone?"

It was a reasonable question, but Oliver had made the mistake of touching Laylee as he spoke, and Laylee looked him over now—his hand on her arm, her gaze strange and frightening in the moonlight—and wondered whether Oliver had lost the whole of his mind. After all, her body was her own business, and she'd not told him he could touch her. The problem was, Oliver wasn't even aware he'd done so.

The ghostly midnight glow had caught the silver in her eyes, and the helmet she wore glinted gold against her skin, and somehow, in that moment, Laylee looked more ethereal than ever: half alive, impossible to grasp, angry even when she smiled. She was a dazzling girl and Oliver Newbanks was in danger of being too thoroughly dazzled. But Laylee could never understand why others were so enchanted by the macabre, or why they found her dance with death so morbidly exciting. It angered her, to be so exoticized.

So she locked eyes with him and said, very quietly, "Not everyone has the right spark, you know."

And pushed him in the snow.

Oliver had mixed feelings about being so unceremoniously shoved to the ground. He was fourteen years old now and fully interested in the sorts of quiet, delicate things that transpired between the hearts of young people, but he never had the chance to sort it all out. By the time he got to his feet and caught up to the others, they'd come upon a large clearing where even the trees knew better than to trespass.

From high above, the scene was spare: a white canvas backdrop painted thick with fresh frost, three winter coats triangulated before a claw-foot tub half-buried in the snow. It was somehow implausibly colder here—as there was a distinct lack of life to lend any heat to the space—and it was silent, desperately silent. Unnervingly so. No living thing—not plant, not insect, not animal—dared disturb the rituals of the final bath, and so they were alone, they three: the strangest sort of children come to hold hands with the dark.

Forgotten for the moment was the cold, the ice, the fear, the hour. Night had been sliced open and, within it, they found mortality. This, the final act of the dead, demanded respect that could not be taught. This was the least alive they'd be tonight, and a hush fell over their reverent forms as three sets of knees hit the ground before dawn. Alice and Oliver had not been told to be still; they were compelled to be. Shadows crept up their limbs, wrapped around their mouths and ears and bones and squeezed. Breaths were extinguished; lips did not move; sounds were not made; and from the silence emerged an understanding: Life would clasp hands with death on these occasions only, in the interest of servicing both worlds and the wandering spirits that belonged therein.

Break this bond, and you, too, shall break.

Alice and Oliver gasped and choked their way back to steady breaths, heaving softly as the shadows lifted, massaging throats and lips and frozen hands. Their wild eyes found each other—for fear had found them first—and they held tight to one another, soundlessly saying all that would remain unspoken.

Laylee sighed, disappointed.

Alice and Oliver would never be true mordeshoors—for that, they'd need the blood—but if they were to ever be even remotely useful, they'd have to first unlearn their fears.

❖

The tub had no spigot, no spout, no knobs or levers, but when Laylee placed her bare, frozen hands on either side of the porcelain, its depths began to fill—slowly at first, and then quickly, furiously, sloshing hard against the edges.

Where the water came from, not even Laylee knew; all that mattered was that it existed. The first fill was always the most heavily perfumed, and the heady aroma was nearly too much for Alice and Oliver, who, bent forward with the weight of its lure, had not yet realized its purpose. The scent, you see, was a siren song for the dead, and the distant sounds of their slogging, dragging limbs meant they'd already begun their pilgrimage to water.

Single file, the decaying corpses cut a swerving path through the snow, occasionally stumbling over their molting limbs, bone shoving through sinew with each inarticulate movement, and Laylee had at least the propriety to look ashamed. (It was, after all, her fault they were falling apart.) She knew she should've dispatched her dead long ago, but it was a hard, thankless job and, well—normally no one was around to judge the state of her subjects.

Alice and Oliver could not mask their disgust.

Laylee took this reaction quite personally, but I really feel I should say—that is, it is my humble opinion that even a band of *newly* dead corpses would've affected them thus. (In fact, I tried telling Laylee this very thing, but she refused to listen. I'm afraid the girl is too hard on herself.)

Laylee, for her part, was watching the bodies closely,

carefully ascertaining when to make their marching stop. For the sake of her guests, she gave them a wide berth, and when they'd reached a ten-foot radius of their little clearing, Laylee held up her hand. No words, just this simple movement, and all forty-six of them collided to a halt, collapsing in a tangled, rotting heap. Laylee cringed as she heard an ankle snap off one man's leg and roll to the ground. This was not the way to show her guests a good time.

Oliver had swallowed back the same bit of bile on no fewer than four occasions now, and Alice, who'd nearly fainted in as many times, was still upstanding simply because the imagined stench arising from the distant pile of flesh had kept her conscious against her will. *This*, she thought, was her reward for performing so well at her Surrender. She could scarcely believe her luck.

Laylee had turned her eyes back to the tub, and Alice, who could bear to look at the mangled limbs no longer, was grateful for the reprieve. A thin layer of ice had already begun to form at the surface of the water, but Laylee broke the ice with a practiced swiftness, and it was this that prompted a newly shivering, nearly vomiting Alice to say,

"Couldn't we possibly move the tub inside?"

But Laylee would not look at her. "You cannot wash the dead where the living still sleep," was all she said.

Alice didn't know how to respond, for fear of saying the

wrong thing. She was beginning to think of Laylee as infinitely more frightening than any dead person she'd ever met, and even Oliver (who was hard-pressed to think rationally when faced with such a beautiful façade), found himself rethinking his attraction to this young mordeshoor. Perhaps it was the stack of putrid bodies piled off to the side, or maybe it was the single finger he'd just discovered in his sleeve, but there was something distinctly unromantic about this experience, and Oliver couldn't yet suss out the why. In fact, he and Alice had just decided that this was quite possibly the worst adventure they'd ever undertaken when Laylee surprised them both by doing something strange and beautiful, and for just a moment, no one could remember to be afraid.

Slowly, very slowly, Laylee had touched her lips. She let her fingers linger at the seam for just a few seconds, and then finally, carefully, she retrieved a single red rose petal from the inside of her mouth.

This she let fall into the tub.

Instantly, the water changed. It was now a boiling, churning sea of liquid crimson, and Alice was so stunned she nearly stumbled, and Oliver, who caught her, was staring at Laylee in shock and awe.

Laylee would not look away from the water. "Choose your first body," she said quietly. "You will have to carry it here yourself."

Alice and Oliver set off at once.

Laylee did not watch them as they went, or she would have seen them stumbling—half fear, half exhilaration—toward the mass of matted bodies, holding fast to each other lest they lose the little courage that kept them warm. No, she was too busy watching the water, combing its ruddy depths with her eyes in search of something—a sign, maybe, that she hadn't made a false move. The thing was, Laylee was beginning to wonder whether an offer of assistance could ever arrive so sincerely. She felt weak of mind and bone, certain now that she'd agreed far too hastily, so desperate for help that she'd lost what good sense she had left.

The longer she stood alone, the more intensely the night gnawed at her. Had she sold herself to a pair of strangers? For what? A few nights' reprieve from the occupation to which she was fettered? Why had she so easily broken? More distressing still:

What would they take from her after she'd taken what she wanted from them?

Laylee had no way of knowing that her fears were unfounded. She knew not the hearts of her two companions, and she'd never have believed a stranger capable of possessing pure intentions. No, she lived in a world where goodness had failed her, where darkness inhaled her, where those she loved had haunted and discarded her. There was no monster, no ghoul, no corpse in a grave that could hurt her the way humans had, and Laylee was afraid that tonight she'd made a most grievous mistake.

So when her companions finally returned, death in their arms and good deeds on their minds, Laylee had once again shuttered closed the doors and windows of her heart. She was no longer merely curt, but now edging on cruel, and she did not care whose heart she hurt, so long as it wasn't hers.

✤

It was Alice who returned first.

She was carrying a small child in her arms—a boy of seven or eight—and she was openly weeping. Forgotten was her innocence, her fear, her childish approach to their solemn business tonight. For it is one thing to behold the dead—and entirely another to hold it. In her arms this child was human, too real, and Alice could not manage her emotions. She was bordering on mild hysteria, and Laylee had no patience for it.

"Wipe your face," she said. "And be quick about it."

"How can you be so unmoved?" said Alice, her voice breaking. Her arms were shaking from the weight she could not carry and, very gently, she let the child's body fall to her feet. "How?" she said again, wiping at her tears. "How can you do this without *feeling*—"

"It's not your place to wonder at what I feel." And Laylee unearthed a small whip (hung from a belt beneath her cloak) and cracked it once through the air.

Alice gasped.

But Laylee did not care. For Alice it was easy to grieve; for Laylee it was nearly impossible. The ghost of the young boy was still very much alive for her, and currently he was prancing about the tub, making crude comments about Alice's face.

Laylee cracked the whip again and the ghost screamed, disintegrating for just a moment. The damage was never permanent, but the whip worked well enough to keep the more ghoulish in line. Laylee cracked the whip just once more—

"Oh, for Feren's sake!" cried Alice.

—and soon the boy's disgruntled spirit was stone-faced and brooding, shooting Laylee dirty looks as he stood by, awaiting his send-off to the Otherwhere.

"Put the body into the tub," Laylee demanded. "Do it now."

Alice swallowed hard, too nervous to be contrary. It took a great deal of effort, but she managed to set aside her tears just long enough to lift the child into the water.

The moment the body hit the liquid, the churning waves were put to peace, and the red water went clear once more.

Alice smiled.

Laylee, meanwhile, had begun clearing a section of snow. From under the drift, she unearthed a large metal chest and unlatched the lid, revealing an assortment of ancient tools. Laylee grabbed several hard-bristled brushes, handed two to Alice, and said, "Now scrub off the filth."

Alice looked up at her, eyes wide with fear. "*What do you mean?*" she whispered.

Laylee nodded to the water. "It looks clean now," she said. "But you'll see what your tears were worth as soon as you're done with him."

The scrubbing of six bodies took just under seven hours. Hands red and raw, fingers frozen, noses numbed beyond all sensation: by the end, all three children were nearly dead themselves. One corpse had been so intensely foul that the shadows had not only clung to him, they'd congealed to form a nearly impenetrable skin, and Oliver had to peel back the darkness one excruciating layer at a time. Alice, for her part, had quickly set aside her fears, reaching instead for fortitude, drawing from an inner well of strength so deep even Laylee took notice. These two strangers were extraordinary in their resolve, uncomplaining through the night, and Laylee was finally beginning to realize that these were not ordinary children. She couldn't help but hope they weren't there to harm her.

❖

The sun switched shifts with the moon.

Weak morning light filtered through a changing sky, golden

violets and dandelion blues offering the first rays of heat to be felt all night. The children's arms were nearly broken with effort—and legs nearly paralyzed by cold—but the work of the evening was still unfinished. Laylee (who, lest we forget, had washed nine bodies of her own not ten hours prior) could hardly move for fatigue, but she made one final effort. Her cold, clumsy hands unearthed a mess of clothespins, and she offered a few shaking fistfuls to both Alice and Oliver. They three worked wordlessly—moving so slowly they might've been wading through warm milk—and hoisted half-sopping, half-frozen bodies onto a hefty clothesline. They pinned hinges to hawser, securing only necks and knees and elbows and the like; once done, dead heads lolled onto stone chests, limp hands flapped against locked wrists, and wet clothes whipped in the brisk morning wind. Six new bodies were strung alongside the nine from the day before, and as the three living children stepped back to admire their work, they fell over sideways and promptly fell asleep in the snow.

Too soon, they were awoken by an eager sun. The golden orb was glittering directly overhead, vibrating warmth with a cheerfulness that seemed remarkably out of place on this brisk afternoon. The snow under the necks and toes of our brave protagonists had melted in gentle waves, each cascade drifting their bodies down a modest slope back toward the castle. Slow, groggy, and drenched to the bone—they blinked open six bleary eyes into the blinding light.

The few birds still in residence had gathered for their daily conference, and Laylee saw them studying her. She groaned and turned away, rubbing her face as she did. They and she seldom spoke to one another, but she knew they pitied her, and this made her resent their airs and upturned beaks, and she could never forgive them for always looking down on her as they flew by. Only once had she climbed a tree tall enough to turn her nose up at *them,* but she'd only the briefest moment to revel in the glory of dim-witted pride before three doves took turns defecating on her head. Remembering this now, she cast a dark look at the birds, wiped imaginary excrement from her helmet, and—still scowling—dragged herself up out of the melted snow.

Meanwhile, Alice and Oliver remained half mired in the slushy filth, disoriented by sleep and forgetting where they were. They finally managed to help each other up, squelching to their feet and squinting in the noon light. Tired, hungry, and urgently requiring a washing, they looked to Laylee for instructions on how best to proceed. They were hoping she would invite them inside—maybe offer them a bit of breakfast or point them in the direction of a warm bath—

Instead, she said, "Come on then," with a tired wave of her hand. "We've got to ship them off before they get soiled again. The bodies are very vulnerable right now."

To say that Alice and Oliver were devastated would've been a gross understatement of the truth—but there was nothing to be done about their discomfort. Alice had agreed to her task, and Oliver had agreed to help Alice, and the both of them had agreed to assist Laylee. So they nodded, gritted their teeth, and staggered forward, sad and sopping in dripping clothes.

Alice and Oliver helped Laylee unclip her dead from the clothesline. The corpses had frozen solid while they slept—icicles hung from their chins and ears and shirt hems—but they'd been defrosting steadily in the sunlight, which made them a bit easier to maneuver. Once unclipped, the heavy bodies fell to the ground with a series of tremendous *thud*s, and Alice and Oliver, who stood stock-still and ankle-deep in dead, were ordered to wait as they were—while Laylee hurried off to retrieve the necessary items for the next steps.

She was gone for some time, rummaging around in her moldy shed of death, and in her absence Alice and Oliver had time to reflect on their horrible evening. Alice was trying to be optimistic, but Oliver was not having it. They'd been swathed in sludge up to their frozen knees, their clammy skin hugged by sodden dress; they were starved, exhausted, filthy even behind their eyeballs—and had now been ordered to keep still amidst a pile of half-melted bodies. Oliver simply refused to see the good in it.

"I can't *believe*," he was saying, "that this is what winning the Surrender got you." He crossed his arms, head shaking. "It's a bad deal, if you ask me. An awful deal."

"But—"

"Maybe," he said, his face brightening, "maybe we could just go home."

"Oliver!" Alice gasped. "How can you say such a thing?"

"Oh, just imagine it! Wouldn't it be lovely to go back?"

"Well *you* are free to go wherever you like," said Alice, who was now plucking a leech off her sleeve. "But I'm not going anywhere. I've a task to accomplish, and I'll do it with or without you, Oliver Newbanks, no matter your whining."

"But don't you see? It's a perfect plan," he said, his eyes aglow. "Your father is a Town Elder now—I'm sure he'd make an exception for you. And you'll just ask for a redo, that's all. I'm sure they'll understand."

"Don't be ridiculous. This is already my second go-around. I haven't any interest in repeating my Surrender again. Besides," Alice sniffed, "they've already made an exception by sending me here; Ferenwood is making a great effort to reform its ties with other magical lands, and Father says it's important I do well here so that we might continue in this direction. And anyway, it's precisely *because* Father is a Town Elder that I need to be on my best behavior. Things have been so wonderful since he's come home and I won't be the one to ruin it for him. No, we'll just need to make do with what we've got and—"

"Make do with what we've got?" Oliver cried. "What have we got, Alice? A pile of dead people and the girl who loves them. Goodness, that doesn't seem like much."

"Why Oliver Newbanks," said Alice, raising an eyebrow. "What a strange thing to say."

"What do you mean?"

"I'm just surprised to hear you speak ill of our hostess." Alice smiled. "I thought you seemed quite taken with her."

At this, Oliver blushed a furious pink.

He fumbled for at least an eighth of a minute and when he

finally spoke he said, "Such—such nonsense, Alice. I haven't any idea what you're talking about."

And at precisely that moment, Laylee came into view.

She was a truly striking girl, even caked in grime, and Oliver Newbanks—who doth protest too much if I do say so myself—could not help but notice. Laylee's eyes were a sensationally bizarre color, and they caught the light like liquid pewter lit by flame. She'd shucked off her helmet only to tuck it under her arm, and the business of doing so had left her a bit disheveled; stray locks of hair had escaped her carefully wrapped headscarf, and the loose tendrils, tipped in silver, lent a softness to her features that was entirely deceptive. She was feeling far from soft as she dragged along a long, flat cart, her face furrowing from the physical effort required to pull its heavy load. She stopped only a moment to wipe at her perspiring brow and, noticing her unkempt hair, quickly tucked the half-silver strands back underneath her scarf. It was only when Alice and Oliver—who'd just remembered their manners—ran forward to help that they saw the wares she'd been hauling: Stacked flat and vertical and packed high to the sky were dozens of simple wooden coffins.

Alice's heart gave a little leap.

Oliver's stomach heaved.

Even so—*even so*—he decided to be chivalrous. Now, it was true that Oliver Newbanks thought Laylee was a beautiful girl. But you must remember: Beauty is easily forgotten in the face of death, decrepitude, and general unpleasantness. So, while, *yes,* Oliver thought Laylee was very pretty (when he had the luxury of thinking such things), that wasn't what moved him now. No, there was something *about* Laylee—something about her Oliver couldn't quite place—that drew him to her, and though at the time he couldn't understand what it was, the explanation was actually quite simple.

Reader, he admired her.

Because somehow, even with the encumbrance of such an unfortunate and isolating occupation, she walked through darkness with elegance, navigating the corridors of life and death with a confidence he'd always secretly longed for. She appeared so self-assured, so steady—so untroubled by the opinions of others—it inspired in him something he'd never experienced before. He was made nervous at the sight of her. He was suddenly eager to understand her. Most of all, he wished she were his friend.

"Please," he said, looking her in the eye. He placed a warm hand atop her tired one as he took the burden over. "Let me do this."

Laylee snatched away her hand and scowled, launching a feeble protest in the process (she didn't *really* want to keep lugging the cart, but her pride would not let her relinquish the load without a struggle), but Oliver would not be moved. Laylee, who had not anticipated any part of this conversation, was so surprised by his insistence that she was rendered, for a moment, speechless. Any help at all was more than she'd ever had, but this was more than she'd expected even from her guests. It was a small gesture, yes—but Laylee was so unused to kindness that even the thinnest acts of consideration soothed the tired heart inside her.

Finally, gratefully, she surrendered.

She and Alice stood together silently as Oliver dragged the heavy cart through the muck, and Laylee looked on in quiet contemplation as his figure shrank into the distance.

"Alice," Laylee said suddenly.

Alice was so stunned to be spoken to that she nearly jumped in place. "Y-yes?" she said.

"What's he worth?"

"Who?" said Alice quickly. "Oliver?"

"Yes. This boy." Laylee nodded toward Oliver's retreating form. "Is he trustworthy?"

"*Trustworthy?*" This, Alice had to think about. "Well," she said carefully. "Yes, I think so."

"You think so?"

"That is—I'm fairly certain. It's just that he used to be the most horrible liar." Alice laughed. "He has the magic of persuasion, you know. Complicates things a bit."

Laylee turned to look at her now, alarmed. *"Persuasion?"*

Alice nodded. "He can make people think and do anything

he wants. And goodness knows"—she laughed again—"he used to be awful about it." But then, noticing the look of horror on Laylee's face, she said quickly, "Oh, but I wouldn't worry about it, really! He's much better now!"

Too late.

Laylee had gone cold. Her eyes went dark; her lips went still. She looked away. She seemed suddenly and inexplicably angry and, taking a deep breath, she clasped her gloved hands together too tightly.

Alice—who'd said exactly the wrong thing—felt Laylee's unexpected moment of friendship slipping away and began to flounder. She knew she had to take advantage of any opportunities to make progress with Laylee; after all, Alice still had no real idea what she was supposed to be doing here, and she was growing desperate. Unfortunately, desperation made her reckless.

"Laylee," she said quickly. "If you would only trust *me*—if you would only tell me what's wrong—"

Laylee stiffened. "Why do you keep insisting that something is wrong with me?"

"No! No—not, not *wrong* with you," said Alice hastily, "just that there might be something *bothering* you." She hesitated, crossed her fingers, and said, "Is there something bothering you? Something you'd like to talk about?"

Laylee looked incredulously at Alice (Laylee was beginning to think Alice was a bit soft in the head) before gesturing across the endless field of dirty, melting snow, its dead bodies and empty caskets, and said, "Something bothering me? What do you think is bothering me? Do you think I enjoy this line of work? Do you think I'm thrilled to be the sole mordeshoor for a land of eighty thousand people?"

"N-no," said Alice, who was already feeling terrified. "But I just thought, perhaps there's something else—some other reason why I was sent here. You see, I have a very particular kind of magic," she rushed on, "and mine isn't much good for washing dead bodies, so I was wondering—"

"Let me be clear," said Laylee, whose expression had gone so cold Alice had to resist the impulse to shudder. "I did not ask you to be here. I did not ask for your help. If you don't want to work—if washing dead bodies is beyond *your particular kind of magic*—you are free to go. In fact," Laylee said carefully, her voice sharp and forbidding, "it might be best if you left right now."

And with that, she charged off into the distance, toward Oliver and her many wooden coffins, and left Alice all alone and heartbroken in the slush.

For Alice Alexis Queensmeadow, things weren't going at all according to plan.

Laylee couldn't be bothered to care.

She was too sensitive to Alice's repeated insinuations that there might be something wrong with her, and it made her cruel and defensive. Laylee threw up new walls, feeling more vulnerable by the moment, and struggled to ignore the sudden, unprecedented tremor in her hands. Still, she marched forward through the sludge, taking in rapid lungfuls of the crisp fresh air, and clenched her fists to keep them steady. Oliver was just up ahead, waiting patiently beside a tall stack of coffins. He caught her eye and smiled, his violet eyes crinkling in delight, and Laylee was so startled by the sight of it she felt something stumble inside of her. It was such a strange, unexpected sensation that for a moment—a very brief moment—Laylee thought she might cry. She wouldn't, of course, but she did solemnly wish she could afford to fall apart every once in a while.

In any case, Laylee did not return Oliver's smile.

She had no interest in untrustworthy, manipulative liars, no matter their claims of reformation. No, there was no chance of her befriending this duplicitous boy or the daft, silly girl. So she flipped open her red cloak—for the first time, Oliver glimpsed the ancient, heavily brocaded silk gown she wore underneath—unhooked an old, nicked, elaborately carved silver crowbar from the tool belt she wore around her waist, and set to work. (On her belt she also carried an old brass mallet; her leather ghost whip; the silky, quilted pouch full of Quicks; a pair of rusty pliers; a copper box full of nails; a branding iron; and a little holder for her business cards.) Silently, she climbed atop the transport and began prying off the wooden lids.

Oliver scrambled up the side of the cart to join her.

From where they stood, Alice was now even more visible: the young Ferenwood girl was standing small and alone in the distance, and she cut a sad, half-slumped figure in the snow. But whatever you might think of Laylee, know this: Her conscience had not yet broken, and it tormented her now perhaps more than ever. Laylee secretly wished she were a normal child—the kind who could make friends and amends all in the same day—but Laylee was simply too wounded herself to know how to undo the hurt she inspired. Her heart, thudding around inside her, was already panicking at the very idea of apologizing to Alice. No, she was too raw, too terrified of rejection to say she was sorry—

Because what if her apologies weren't accepted?

What if she made herself vulnerable only to have her faults thrown back in her face?

No, no, it was safer to stay angry, she'd concluded, where nothing could ever touch her.

Luckily, Oliver had no such scruples.

He cleared his throat and said, as carefully as possible, "Why, um—why is Alice standing all the way over there?"

Laylee had already pried the lids off several coffins by the time Oliver asked his question, so she was breathing hard and hauling open caskets onto the snow when she said, "I told her that if she didn't like this line of work, she should leave."

Oliver froze in place, stunned. "Why in heavens would you do that?"

Laylee shrugged. "She said her magic wasn't suited to washing dead bodies."

"But—Laylee—"

"And anyway she keeps demanding to know what's wrong with me—as though I'm a nut to be cracked." Laylee dragged down another casket, exhaling a sharp breath. "But there is nothing the matter with me." She looked up to meet Oliver's eyes as she said this, but once she stopped moving, her hands— visibly shaking—belied her words.

Laylee pretended not to notice and moved quickly to reach

for another coffin, but Oliver had the good sense to stop her. "If there's nothing the matter with you," he said, "then what's wrong with your hands?"

"Nothing," she snapped, closing her trembling fingers into fists. "I'm tired, that's all. We had a very long night."

Oliver faltered—for he could not deny that this was true—and finally relented with a sad sigh. "All Alice wants is to help you," he said.

"Then she should be over here *helping*," said Laylee.

"But you just said you told her not to."

"When someone really wants something," Laylee said, dragging another coffin to the ground, "they'll fight for it. She does not appear to be much of a fighter."

Oliver laughed out loud and looked away, shaking his head in the direction of the sun. "Only someone who didn't know Alice *at all* could say something like that."

Laylee did not respond.

"Goodness," Oliver said, now squinting across the field at Alice's lonely figure. "I can only imagine how thoroughly you broke her heart."

Now Laylee looked at him. Glared at him. Angrily, she said, "If what I said broke her heart, then her heart is too easily broken."

Oliver cocked his head, smiled, and said, "Not everyone is as strong as you are, you know."

At this, Laylee went numb.

"You misunderstand me entirely," she said quietly. "I'm not strong at all."

Oliver, who understood at once the depth of this confession, never had a chance to respond. He was still searching for the right thing to say when Laylee went abruptly rigid—her spine ramrod straight—and inhaled a short, sharp gasp as her crowbar fell, with a dull splash, into the slush. Laylee's legs buckled beneath her and she staggered sideways, toppling into Oliver, who'd come running forward to help, and though he pulled the mordeshoor to her feet, fear and panic were colliding in his eyes, and he cried out for Alice as Laylee shook in her skin. And in the fraction of a second Laylee made the mistake of meeting his gaze, Oliver had looked too long—and learned too much.

Something was desperately wrong.

❖

Alice was now charging toward them—her face fraught with terror as her long, pale hair tossed around in the wind—and Oliver sank to his knees as he searched Laylee's face for signs of trauma.

For a girl so unaccustomed to company, it was a curious, terrifying sensation to be so intimately held—but this matter of physical closeness was a mere trifle on Laylee's long list of concerns. The thing was, she didn't trust these odd children, and she couldn't help but feel that the timing of their arrival, their absurd demands to help her, and her sudden, unbidden frailty had coincided in a way that was more than a little suspicious. She was *not,* as you might have expected, particularly moved by their compassionate faces, and she would not allow herself to be romanced by any moment that demanded she be weak—not here and not now—and especially not while in the company of those whose hearts and minds she still doubted.

So she did the only sensible thing she could think of: As her motor skills were slowly returned to her, she mustered what little strength she had left and ripped herself free of Oliver's embrace. Half dragging, half stumbling, she ran home—paying no mind to Oliver's stunned cries or Alice's shouts of surprise—and, collapsing as she crossed the threshold, she locked the heavy wooden door behind her, leaving the tortured pair of Ferenwoodians in her wake.

Alice and Oliver pounded against her door
for at least a dozen minutes before their throats went raw
from shouting and their fists were bruised by the effort. Finally, fatigue and defeat collapsed into one complicated failure,
and silence flooded the halls of Laylee's home. Relieved, chest
heaving, Laylee finally made an effort to move. But in the time
it took her to get to her feet, the peace was split open by a series
of piercing screams.

Maman was in a right state.

Her disappearance the night before was owed to her cow-
ardliness and nothing more; Maman's fragile spirit had been
frightened by the disturbance of strangers, and so she'd hidden
instead of helped, and now she'd reemerged, more irritated and
more impossible than ever. Let us remember that Maman was
visible only to Laylee (who'd not shared her spirit-speaking
abilities with a single living soul) and, as a result, no one could
see *or* hear what was happening to her now—not even Alice

and Oliver, who'd pressed their tired ears against her door, hoping for a sound of life.

Sadly, only the dead were making any noise at the moment, and it was all Laylee could do to keep from screaming out loud. Maman had cornered her, screeching and wailing about the state of Laylee's filthy clothes.

This last bit was difficult to ignore.

All three children were exceptionally filthy. Not only had they spent the night scrubbing corpses, but they'd then promptly fallen asleep in the waist-deep snow. They'd been mucked up and melted on, and—though she couldn't have known it at the time—Laylee had fallen asleep on a small family of spiders, and their broken legs were still caught in her eyelashes. It was a small mercy then that Laylee had been too preoccupied to welcome her guests inside or offer them something to eat; had she done so, Alice—who'd just picked a fingernail out of her ear—might've arranged the contents of her stomach all over the poor girl's floor.

But Alice and Oliver were either too exhausted or too afraid to pursue Laylee any further. Oliver wouldn't dare break another bedroom window, nor could he bring himself to use his magic against her. Heartbroken, he'd given up entirely, slumping to the ground behind Laylee's door and saying nothing at all, only occasionally shooting dejected, harried glances at Alice instead of speaking aloud his fears. No, he couldn't have known how awful Laylee was feeling, or how terribly Maman was torturing her at that moment.

"Filthy, useless, *foul* girl—"

Laylee clapped her hands over her ears.

"—nasty hands, nasty hands, blistered fingers and broken skin—"

Laylee squeezed her eyes shut.

"—never raised you to be this way, to live like an animal, never clean, never clean—"

Alice had managed to peek through a part in one of the window's curtains, but Laylee's furrowed brows and pinched lips were impossible to understand. In fact, Alice, a decidedly tender girl, couldn't help but wonder if perhaps she and Oliver were the problem—

"Hiring strangers to stay the night, too weak to do the work yourself—"

—and though they were indeed a small part of the suffering, they were actually a very important part of the solution. They just didn't know how much.

❖

Laylee was usually better prepared for Maman's insults. Most days she could handle the onslaught of anger, the violent humiliation, the accusations of incompetence. But Laylee hadn't slept more than a wink in thirty-six hours, and she was collapsing from the inside out. Her body was beaten, her mind was broken, and now her spirit, too, was beginning to fray. Laylee Layla Fenjoon was stronger than most, wiser than some, and absolutely, unequivocally ancient for her age. But even the strong and the wise and the ancient have faltered without compassion or companion, and while Baba had madness and Maman had nonsense, Laylee, in their absence, had locked hands with loneliness, darkness feeding darkness until all light was lost. She could no longer remember what it was like to live without a broken heart.

It was unfortunate, then, that she saw little value in the company of her strange guests. In them she might have found friendship; instead she found fault and reason to fear, and so she spared them no thought as she abruptly abandoned them. Wordlessly, she charged up the castle stairs, locked herself in the toilet, turned on the water, and fell sideways into the tub—where she would remain for some time. She didn't care what happened to Alice and Oliver. In fact, she secretly hoped they'd be gone before she returned.

❖

Dear reader: Laylee would one day look back on these early moments with Alice and Oliver with heartbreaking regret— a remorse so parasitic it would follow her forever. But she needn't be so hard on herself. It is, after all, a simple and tragic thing that on occasion our unkindness to others is actually a desperate effort to be kind to ourselves. I remind her of this even as I write to you now, but still, she struggles. How very important and infuriating it is to have to remind a smart person not to be so stupid as to give up on themselves.

TERRIBLY SAD,
THIS STORY

Alice and Oliver weren't sure what to do.

Oliver was certain that something was very wrong with the young mordeshoor, but he couldn't be exactly sure what the matter was, and anyway, Alice was more frustrated than Oliver, because helping Laylee was *her* task to undertake and she was turning out to be quite bad at it. To make matters worse, the both of them were just about rotting away in their soggy clothes, their skin so clammy with damp that Oliver was beginning to wonder whether his limbs hadn't been slathered in cold pea soup. Everything hurt: toes, teeth, joints, and eyeballs. They were exhausted and overwhelmed, tired of schlepping through corpse droppings and desperate for a change of dress and a bite of something warm.

Still, they were strangers in a strange town—and there was much to be disoriented by. What to do?

Alice had been sent here, to this land of cold and death, as a reward for a Surrender well-done. She was a singularly talented young girl, gifted with a magical skill the Ferenwood

Elders had never seen before, and though it took them some time to decide where, exactly, they should send her to do a bit of good in the world, in the end she was sent to Laylee with little explanation. This lack of explanation was not without intention—it was in fact a direct response to her very high score. Alice would have to be clever enough to sort out her path, her task, *and* its solution—all on her own. (Oliver, it should be noted, had not been allowed to accompany her, but the two of them had been in cahoots for so long now that they paid little attention to laws and their consequences.)

But Alice's earlier optimism was quickly disintegrating, and despite ample evidence that Laylee was in dire straits, Alice found herself grasping for a loophole that might deliver her safely back to Ferenwood—and to Father, who, as Oliver noted, was a Town Elder who might be able to smooth things over. It wasn't a proud moment for Alice, but Laylee had turned out to be prickly and rude and not at all what Alice had expected.

Even so—

The thing was, Alice had earned a 5 on her Surrender— the highest score possible—and she should have anticipated the levels of difficulty and nuance her task would involve. But none of that seemed to matter now. Laylee had insulted Alice and shut her out entirely, and Alice felt she'd suffered enough. She and Oliver (who was already too eager to eject himself from the madness) were now happily acquiescing to cowardice and entirely willing to give up and go home.* In fact, in a desperate bid to rationalize an abrupt exit, it suddenly occurred to Alice that there was quite a lot of sense in Laylee having abandoned them. *Maybe,* she thought, they were no longer needed. Maybe this was the official end of it all. Maybe Alice's task here had nothing to do with her talent—in fact, maybe that was the twist all along.

Could it be? Was this all she'd been tasked to do?

Perhaps—

Perhaps they'd done their bit and should now set off for home? Their challenge had, admittedly, seemed too simple by Alice's usual standards for adventure, but she supposed spending the evening scrubbing filth from the folds of corpses was enough excitement for one lifetime. Alice shared her ignoble

---

* A note: This was a strange departure from the fearless, indefatigable protagonists I knew and loved in *Furthermore***, and I can't say I wasn't surprised when I heard what happened. But we must remember that Oliver had little to gain at the onset of this adventure, and Alice, whose father was now safely home (this will make more sense once you've read *Furthermore*), was eager to get back to her new, happy life. Indeed, neither Alice nor Oliver felt great inclination to put themselves in (excessive) danger for a stranger, and when their discomfort had grown to be too much, they were ready to set sail for home. It was sad, yes—but you see now that Laylee wasn't wrong to have doubted them. The truth was that while their intentions were good, they weren't *pure*; no, Alice's and Oliver's concern for Laylee was motivated by the promise of glory and a bit of good fun, respectively. And it was precisely this kind of selfish motive that Alice and Oliver would have to learn to shed. Help, after all, is at its best when offered unconditionally—with no expectations of payment in return.

**Apologies: *Furthermore* is an altogether different story, one that takes place before this one, wherein Alice and Oliver are the sole protagonists. It's quite good, I think.

thoughts with Oliver, who responded swiftly and with great conviction—

"Oh, I sincerely doubt it."

"But why?" she said, pulling a cockroach out of her hair. "It was awful enough, wasn't it? That could've been the whole of it, don't you think?"

Oliver crossed his arms. "Now, Alice, if you want to give up and head home, you know you have my hearty consent. But you can't *also* pretend you've done what you came here to do. You know full well that there's something the matter with Laylee—something worse than her mordeshoor business— and we've done nothing at all to help her."

"Sure we did," Alice tried to protest. "We washed all those dead people and—"

Oliver shook his head. "You're missing the point. Tasks are always assigned based on *talent*. And you've not used yours at all."

Alice stared at her feet, hugging herself against the cold. "And there are never any exceptions to that rule . . . ?"

"I think you already know the answer to that question."

Alice bit her lip. It was true. She sighed, and with a sad sort of resignation, she said, "So what should we do?"

"Well," said Oliver, "if we're going to stay here and see this through, the very first thing we need to do"—he shook a few worms out of his shoe—"is find a way to get clean. Second, we'll need an entirely new set of clothes." Oliver leaned in and lowered his voice. "I plan to burn this lot"—he gestured to himself—"as soon as it's off. I suggest you do the same."

Alice nodded so vigorously a beetle flew out of her nose.

Now, for a bit of explanation:

Alice and Oliver had traveled to Whichwood via magic, but the decadence could have been dispensed with if they had only been interested in a very long walk. Whichwood was a mere thirty-day hike from Ferenwood, which—had either town ever heard of such absurd inventions as airplanes—would've made it an easy five-hour flight. As it was, Alice and Oliver had had to travel for days by underwater elevator (the worst possible way to travel), as Whichwood was a town older and slower than even Ferenwood, and they'd not updated their modes of transportation into and out of the city in nearly a century.

It should also be stated that every magical land (of which there were many) had its own invented reasons for its bureaucratic solitude, and the people of Whichwood were no different: They wouldn't leave their land for fear of ancient superstition.

Whichwoodians believed that non-magical people had lost their magic as a result of a pervasive, contagious disease, and the only way to save themselves from that terrible fate was to remain forever quarantined from the infected majority. All magical lands imposed barriers that kept the *dizzies* (this was slang for the non-magical "diseased") from discovering their world, but Whichwoodians took this responsibility even a step further: There were no ways into or out of Whichwood except by water, and it was an arduous, extensive journey that few, if any, undertook. As a result, Whichwood was almost entirely forgotten, which was exactly how they preferred it.

In any case, their fair township had everything it needed and wanted for nothing, so the people stayed within the confines of their own creations, never mixing with the dizzies for fear of being infected by their illness, and always suspicious, even of other magical folk. Their heavy suspicion made them appear an unwelcoming lot, but this was only partly true. The truth was that they were a lively, cultured sort of people—when you got to know them—who felt they had a great deal to be afraid of; it was this last bit—this certainty of fear—that helped substantiate the paranoia that demanded their isolation.

It was an illogic they shared with Ferenwood.

The people of Ferenwood, you see, had once upon a time

suffered a great and bloody ordeal at the hands of a neighboring magical land (the ordeal being a result of extensive dealings with non-magicals), and were now sheltered to the point of asphyxiation. The Ferenwood Town Elders had decided long ago that caution and caution alone would keep them from further catastrophe, and so the residents of Ferenwood remained, for the most part, happily unaware of their excised freedoms, until one day their village would break this code of solitude to send a thirteen-year-old girl through sea and snow to do a bit of friendly magic.

It was a decision they would soon regret.

❖

For now, their ambassador in Whichwood was ambling through snowy fields—occasionally tripping, often stumbling—as she and her illegal companion searched for an outlet into town. Alice had been sent with no further instruction than to find Laylee, do what she could to help her, and return home before the snow melted on the ground. But Alice was beginning to think the Elders had cruelly withheld several critical details, as already she was at a loss. Alice had no idea how she was meant to help Laylee; she had no idea how long the snow would stay on the ground; and, more terrifying still, she had no idea how she'd find her way back to Ferenwood.

Their arrival by elevator had been underwhelming at best: The little glass travel box had never been very reliable, but upon reaching its final destination, it gave one final heave and shattered under pressure. (It was a very, very old system.) Alice and Oliver were unceremoniously ejected into the icy seas crashing along the coast of Laylee's castle and emerged sopping wet and scandalized, half-bitten by frost and nearly dead standing up. It was the painful finish of a long and numbing journey, and it was this, their frozen, exhausted desperation, that had prompted Oliver to break Laylee's window in order to take refuge from the cold.

It had been a rough week for the two friends, who'd spent the first five days traveling by wet elevator, and the last scrubbing filth from dead bodies. They were hungry, dirty, and desperate for sleep (careful readers will note that the rules for eating and sleeping were the same in Whichwood as they were in Ferenwood), and they'd seen nothing of town nor country but Laylee's ghostly castle and its bloated corpses. It was not an ideal introduction.

But Alice and Oliver had just remembered something important: that they were skilled, clever, able-bodied young people, and that they'd been through much worse when they were younger and dimmer and (one of them) missing an arm. (Indeed, anyone who remembers Alice and Oliver's adventures in Furthermore could never doubt them now!) So it was then, as they staggered sideways in the snow, anxious and delirious, that they spied a distant road occasionally traveled and, heady with relief, charged blindly into possibility.

Benyamin Felankasak was bothering no one at all—was a hindrance to no one at all—when his steady life was tipped sideways and its contents spilled into the street. He was a gentle, mild-mannered boy of exactly thirteen and three-quarters who split his time between school and the seasonal saffron harvests, and at precisely the moment his troubles truly began, he was wheeling a barrow of saffron flowers along a deserted country road. The crop had been rich this year, and though Benyamin had only a small field to work, he'd managed to harvest quite a lot more than he could carry. The soft, elegant purple flowers were striking against the snowdrift, and though he'd no shoes on his feet nor gloves on his hands, he was one of those rare creatures with a flair for gratitude, and so he smiled despite the cold, thankful for the business that would sustain his family.

Benyamin took this route every Sunday at precisely the same hour. Come saffron or snow, he walked into the train station always after lunch, always after tucking his mother back into bed—where she would remain until Benyamin returned—and after he'd put the house to rights. He knew this road and its wanderers with perfect familiarity, which meant he always knew exactly who and what to expect—which meant he knew better than to expect any kind of stranger in the land of Whichwood. It was this strength of conviction that would cause him such distress today.

Not moments after whispered words of gratitude left his lips were his cart and self knocked into by an unexpected stranger, and Benyamin was lifted out of himself in shock. That his head struck stone, that his spirits were clobbered—this was no matter at all to him. But that the barrow was flung sideways and upside down in the snow, crushing half his harvest in the process? Benyamin was devastated.

He looked up—head pounding, heart pounding—into the eyes of his assailant, and found a face so extraordinarily unlike his own that Benyamin was certain he had died. He sat up slowly, his vision coming in and out of focus, and *yes*—that he was dead he was certain, because he was looking into the eyes of an angel.

She was white as the snow itself. Her skin, her hair, her eyelashes—so extraordinary. An angel, he thought. *Definitely* an angel. And he began searching for her wings.

"Are you alright?" she was saying to him, over and over again. "Are you okay?" She shook him, looked away, looked at someone else. "Oh, Oliver, what have I done?" she cried. "Have I killed him? Have I—"

"Where are your wings?" Benyamin heard himself say to her. His head was spinning more quickly now, but he managed to pull himself into a seated position. Death was blurrier than he thought it would be. "I thought you would have wings," he tried again.

Alice Alexis Queensmeadow was both relieved and confused. She had not killed this innocent boy, but she had apparently done something to his brain. Which was the worse, she did not know.

It was Oliver who pulled Benyamin to his feet and, not a moment later, it was Oliver who let go of his arm with a startled cry, dropping Benyamin to the ground so suddenly that the poor boy knocked his head again. Luckily, the second knock seemed to cure him, and it was just as the fog cleared that Benyamin heard Oliver shout,

"Well, what was I supposed to do? He's covered in spiders! And—and—all kinds of insects! Crawling down his sleeves and scurrying up his legs"—Oliver dropped his face into his hands in horror—"oh, for Feren's *sake,* what have we gotten ourselves into in this mad, hateful town with all these strange, disgusting people—"

"I'm very sorry about the insects," Benyamin said curtly, and Oliver's mouth snapped shut. A blotchy redness spread across his cheeks, and he had at least the decency to look ashamed.

Benyamin, meanwhile, had pulled himself up with great and solemn dignity and stood before them now, not quite as tall as Oliver, but nearly so, and fully comprehending the situation. First: one glance told him his harvest was not beyond saving. Second: that he was not yet dead. And third: Alice—though he did not know her name at the time—was not an angel, no, but a *girl,* and this was perhaps the more miraculous alternative. As a girl, you see, she was the most astonishing he'd ever beheld. She was quite perfect in his estimation, more exquisite than even his saffron flowers, which he loved so dearly. It was only because of Alice, who stood by silently, staring at her feet, that Oliver's words had not injured him. He felt that her heart, quietly tripping in the cold, was a kindred one, and he could not explain the why.

In any case, there was much to be said between these three, and Benyamin was arranging to say it; they had not only the matter of the fallen saffron to discuss, but also the business of *Who are you* and *What are you doing here* to contend with, and though everyone was ready to engage in these productive conversations, they were delayed by yet another unexpected stranger.

A peacock spider had scuttled, unnoticed, up Alice's skirts

and across her coat and around her neck until he sat primly atop her nose, where he had the best position of inspecting her. He flapped his colorful, iridescent fan as he danced sideways across her face, taking eerily elegant steps that made his small, colorful body glitter in the sunlight. The spider was a handsome, clever little creature who'd always been proud of his vivid good looks, so he was curious about Alice and her missing colors, and, being fond of Benyamin, he was hoping to investigate the situation on the boy's behalf.

Meanwhile, Alice was as brave as she could manage as she stood, still and terrified, waiting for the spider to be done with her. She did not yet know how this creature was connected to Benyamin, but she felt there must be a connection between the two, and so she said nothing, unwilling to insult Benyamin any further and silently hating Oliver for having been so rude to this boy in the first place. After all, it was their fault they'd toppled into him.

Even so—

It was all very, very strange.

The residents of Whichwood, much like the residents of Ferenwood, each had a magical talent, but the differences between the two towns (of which there were many) were becoming clearer. In Ferenwood, all citizens Surrendered their talents; they openly celebrated magic and their magical abilities, seldom hiding what they were destined to be. But here in Whichwood, Alice and Oliver had unwittingly stumbled upon a second keeper of secrets in as many days. Benyamin, like Laylee, kept much of his magic to himself, for he never spoke of his relationship with the entomological world, not even to explain away his many-legged entourage. No one seemed to know why he was always covered in insects, not even his mother, and he didn't care to clarify.

The thing was, Benyamin thought humans were strange. He couldn't understand why we wear skin to hide our skeletons and, consequently, he had great respect for those who wore their bones with pride. And though Benyamin identified as human, he took refuge in a small hope that he was at least not as human as the rest of us. This peculiar fantasy was perhaps a result of an incident in his childhood, when Benyamin had scratched an itch until it burst open, emancipating hundreds of newborn spiders from the soft underside of his elbow. He hadn't known until that moment that anything had taken up residence inside of him, and it was only then that he understood what no one else had been able to explain.

For years Benyamin had suffered from a faint, incessant internal itching, and though he oft spoke of it, his torment was never taken seriously. No doctor alive (magical or otherwise) had suspected the invisible itching was the consequence of many little legs scurrying through the veins that bored through him. He was eight years old when his skin first split open, and as he listened to the many tearful good-byes—orphan children leaving home for the first time—Benyamin felt a curious sense of responsibility over these alien creatures. From then on, whenever a new family burst forth from his flesh, he sent them off into the world with all the tenderness of a loving father.

At thirteen and three-quarters years old, Benyamin was the strangest boy Alice would ever know, and this first meeting was the beginning of everything. Benyamin, who was highly aware of his oddness, had never known anyone who might match him in his strangeness, and meeting Alice was, for him, an act of fate. That anyone should surprise him was entirely refreshing, and it was for this reason alone that he didn't call away his eager spider friend. He was curious to see Alice's reaction, and her studied calm, her stubborn dignity, and above all, her gentle heart—in the face of what was so obviously a fear—left an indelible impression on him; though he had little interest in Oliver—whom he saw only as her rude companion—Benyamin had now more questions than ever. Who was she, this prismatic girl? Why was she here? Would she stay forever? But he could not bring himself to be so bold. For now, he could only steal glances.

Alice had plucked the spider off her nose (she'd finally grown tired of being stared at) and set him on the ground, and the spider was so tremendously excited by the experience that Benyamin was forced to laugh against his will. Oliver, eager to erase the earlier ugliness, took advantage of the moment and stepped forward earnestly—apologizing all at once—and, though altogether ineloquent, his intentions were understood. Benyamin smiled more certainly this time, and though he did not say a word, he shook his head as if to say, *That's perfectly alright. You look like a bit of an idiot anyway.*

And Oliver was grateful.

It was the start of a very valuable friendship.

Now let us return to our mordeshoor.

Laylee, you will remember, was still locked in the toilet. She was lying on her back, floating fully dressed in the claw-foot tub, her sodden clothes splayed like molted wings. She'd so overfilled the tub that water sloshed down its porcelain skin with her every move, flooding the small bathroom that was her only refuge.

But Laylee was too preoccupied to notice.

She stared only at the ceiling, counting moths to keep from weeping, and inhaled in short, sharp breaths as her heart creaked in her chest. With shaking hands, she felt for her damaged bones and let out a soft cry; her small shoulders had dented under the weight of too much responsibility, and she could feel the disfiguration through her clothes. With fumbling, trembling fingers, she unlatched her golden cuffs, anklets, and chest plate, and heaved the lot of them out of the water and onto the cracked, patinated marble floor, where they landed with a tremendous clatter. Laylee flinched at the sound but could not be moved to care more.

These ancient ornaments—what good were they now? They were from a time long, long ago, when mordeshoor blood was so royal it bled blue in the snow. No, this drafty castle, these faded clothes—she picked at the chipped sapphires sewn onto her gown—were from a lost century. There was no longer any pride in being a mordeshoor. No pomp, no circumstance, no decadence in dying. And now, as she traced the blue veins snaking under her skin, Laylee laughed at how much life she'd sacrificed for death.

She closed her eyes and laughed harder as she dropped below the surface, the water garbling the happy sounds into something strange and terrifying, her eerie gales echoing across the arched ceilings. Laylee shivered uncontrollably, even as the hot water scalded her skin, and suddenly she froze—eyes wide with terror—and sat up in one swift, jerky movement, throat choking, bent over coughing, and gripped the tub with silver hands.

The long and terrible evening had taken its toll.

It was only after she'd abandoned Alice and Oliver that Laylee discovered her hands had gone fully silver; indeed, she'd been so distraught by the revelation that she'd tipped sideways into the still-filling tub and had remained supine ever since. She lifted her arms now, horrified and fascinated, to watch as the thin gray tongues crept up her wrists, claiming her one lick at a time.

Laylee had always thought she was ready for death. She, a mordeshoor by blood, had thought she'd overcome the fears of nonexistence. But Laylee was only now beginning to understand: It was not death she feared as much as she feared *dying*; it was this, her powerlessness in the face of mortality that unscrewed her courage from its sticking place.

Still, it was unusual—

The longer Laylee stared at the creeping sickness, the calmer she became. The moment of death felt now more imminent than ever, and Laylee was reassured by one simple certainty: that the pain, the suffering, and the unceasing loneliness would at least be over soon enough. The illness, you see, appeared to be consuming her at an exponential rate. Laylee would be dead by the end of the week, and there was nothing she could do to slow it down.

Sadly, it was only this—the horrible promise of relief—that could soothe her shaking limbs, and soon Laylee was able to thaw and exhale, to continue existing just long enough to shed this last skin of humanity.

Her unwelcome helpers had arrived just a touch too late.

Laylee heaved herself up, sopping wet and weighted down, and began to peel off wet layers of clothing. Everything she owned in the world was inherited from someone already dead. Her gowns and cloaks and boots and scarves were sourced from Maman and Grandmaman—they were pieces from another era, fashionable long before Laylee was born. Everything she owned—from doorknobs to dinner plates—was little more than a token of a lost world. She let each piece of wet clothing fall into the tub with a terrific *splash*, pulled the cork from the drain, wrapped herself in the bath mat, tiptoed into her room, and—

Oh.

Laylee had nearly forgotten.

Oliver, good friend that he was, had broken her bedroom window.

✦

In all the hours Laylee had been gone, the wind and snow had thrashed about her private quarters with a desperate savageness. Icicles had been born along her shattered window-panes; fingers of frost curled into delicate fists around objects tall and wide. Flurries collected in haphazard piles, half-melted flakes snaking water across her floors in skeletal patterns. She raked her nails through a layer of ice coating her single mirror and shuddered. It was unmercifully cold in these drafty quarters, and Laylee shivered on tiptoe, her muscles seizing. With shaking hands, she yanked a set of clean, moth-eaten clothes out of a warped, wheezing armoire, and tugged on infinite layers of ancient fabric.

Thick, shimmering silver stockings irreparably torn at both knees and poorly mended at the toes. A layered set of angora turtlenecks tucked into a pair of faded, fleece-lined turquoise pants. A heavy, ruby-encrusted, floor-length gown to be worn atop it all—its carefully embroidered sleeves torn at the elbows, old blood smeared across the bodice, six diamond buttons missing down the back—and a stained feather vest cinched at the waist with a string of old pearls. Finally, Laylee locked her soggy tool belt around her hips and stepped into a pair of purple work boots, dirt and blood baked into their delicate silk flesh.

Laylee had tried to sell her family heirlooms countless times, but no one in this superstitious town would buy the belongings of a mordeshoor, no matter their gold stitches or sapphires. And so she starved quietly, died slowly, and cried when no one was looking—this girl who could not help but wear diamonds as she buried her dead.

Laylee took a steadying breath.

She secured a fresh scarf over her head, fastened her red cloak over her shoulders, and made a decision.

She'd drowned her pride in the tub and left it there to die— and good riddance, too—because she was about to do something her pride never would've allowed.

She was going to ask for help.

Her strangers were too late to help *her,* of this she was sure, but they might not be too late to help the town. If Laylee could only convince Alice and Oliver to come back, they could perhaps dispatch the rest of the dead before it was too late. Laylee's death, you see, would cause more devastation in Whichwood than anyone had bothered to realize. The foolish denizens of her town had left her to fend for herself—she was young and female and all alone, and she'd become an easy target for the stingy and the sexist and the cruel among her people—and they'd cheated her out of honest earnings, knowing full well that her blood made it so she had no choice but to take on the work.

It wasn't always like this.

Mordeshoors used to mean something in Whichwood. They used to matter. But people had gotten used to abusing Laylee, and they'd lost sight of the risks—the consequences—of defrauding a mordeshoor.

They'd forgotten the ancient rhyme.

You'd try to cheat a mordeshoor?
You'd dishonor this noble deed?
What comes of all this wickedness?
Filthy swindlers!
Take heed:
A gentle warning to remind you
Of the things that you've forgot
Your mortal skin
will slowly thin
Your heart will fail and rot.
Steal from any mordeshoor!
And walk free for just a day.
Steal from any mordeshoor!
And death will make you pay.

Let me explain:

There could never elapse more than three months between a death and its spirit's dispatch to the Otherwhere. Any longer than that, and the souls grew too attached to this world and would do whatever they could to stay.

This was what had happened to Maman.

Baba (from whom Laylee had inherited her magic as a mordeshoor) had been too distraught to wash Maman's lifeless body and, under the pretense of finding (and fighting) Death itself, had left home and was led eternally astray by grief. Laylee, only eleven years old at the time, hadn't known what to do. She'd only trained with Baba a short while before he left, and had been understandably horrified by the idea of washing her own mother's decaying corpse—never mind the fact that she could barely lift the woman into a tub. So she did what anyone would've done in her situation: She ignored the problem and hoped it would go away on its own.

But the doorbell kept ringing.

Corpses piled up faster than she could count them, and it was all Laylee could do to drag them into her shed and keep them sheltered until Baba came home. At first she did nothing but wait—but within a month she was out of food and out of options, and soon she was scrubbing as many dead as she was able and taking whatever money she was offered. She threw herself into her work, washing bodies until her fingers bled, determined to direct her mounting fury into something productive. But every night, no matter the weather, she'd steal away from Maman's angry ghost and sleep outside in the open air, her young heart still soft enough to hope. She thought maybe Baba had forgotten she was in there, and she prayed he would see her waiting for him if he ever passed by. She held on to hope for six months before she discovered him in town one day, counting his teeth in the middle of the street. He'd been selling them in exchange for food. It was only then that Laylee gave up on the world she'd once loved. That was when—at eleven and one half years old— she finally washed her mother's rotted dead body and, ready to send her off, had discovered Maman's spirit would not be moved. Maman's ghost had grown too attached to this world, and she wouldn't be persuaded to leave her daughter, no matter the tears Laylee shed.*

The problem was, there were rules about ghosts who wanted to stay behind. Life and death were regulated by endless bureaucracy, and exceptions to the system could not be made without proper procedure. Spirits were, first of all, deeply discouraged from remaining in the land of the living (for a long list of reasons I won't bore you with now), but those ghosts who insisted on living with mortals would have to find a mortal skin to wear. Without it, a spirit would eventually disintegrate, dissolved of both life and death forever, the worst of all possible fates.

Any skin would do, really, but human skin was the spirits'

---

* To be clear: That Maman was *unkind* to Laylee was not actually her fault. Maman was entirely unaware of her bad temper and sharp tongue. She was simply made of a different kind of stardust now, the kind that made her, by default, a dark, pessimistic, biting sort of creature. Still, she loved her daughter to a fault.

favorite, as it had the best fit and that *je ne sais quoi*—nostalgia, perhaps?—that reminded them of better times.* If all this sounds terrifying—don't worry: It was the job of Laylee (and people like her) to prevent it from ever happening. This was precisely why it was so important to pay a mordeshoor a living wage. Dead mordeshoors, you will understand, could only do so much.

And everything had a schedule.

After three months, the magic that bound ghosts to their mordeshoor would break, and they would then be free to leave hallowed ground, roam the land, and steal skins from the first persons they could find.

Ticktock.

It was coming up on days eighty-seven, eighty-eight, and eighty-nine for all of Laylee's dead, which meant the people of Whichwood were running out of time.

---

* Maman, you will note, was protected from this unfortunate condition on account of her blood relation to her daughter, a living mordeshoor. Mordeshoors always straddled the line between the living and the dead, and they were welcome in either world, in any form, at any time.

It might not surprise you to hear that, for practical purposes, a portion of Laylee's vast property had been landscaped to accommodate an ancient, overcrowded cemetery. But it *might* surprise you to hear that the citizens of Whichwood cared very little for this cemetery, and that they were a people who did not visit their dead. Mourners rarely came by Laylee's freshly planted graves to lay flowers or have tearful conversations with the memories of their loved ones, and this was because the Whichwoodians were—as I mentioned earlier—an extremely superstitious people, who believed that being kind to the dead would only encourage the cold corpses to come back to life. So, as they had no great desire to have their lives rampaged by festering zombies, they were content to leave the dead undisturbed. This meant that the ghosts who lived on Laylee's land had little distraction from their tedious ghost schedules, and as the hours of the day dragged on long and dull, seeing Laylee never ceased to please them. For the ghosts she served, Laylee was a *delight*.

But as she stepped out onto the land to collect her fallen helmet and crowbar, Laylee remembered what she'd nearly forgotten: She'd left the morning's work unfinished—and the ghosts had no problem reminding her. In an instant, a school of gauzy wisps were screeching her name.

Laylee looked up with a reluctant smile as fifteen spirits sidled up to her. She gave her ghosts a limp wave. "Hi," she said, scooping up her wet helmet in the process. "How is everyone?" She shoved the helmet onto her head and stifled a shudder as a dollop of cold slush slid down her forehead.

"Good," the ghosts chorused, all flat and monotone.

"We've been sharing our death stories again," said Zahra, looking gloomy.

"And Roksana was telling us her theories about the Otherwhere," said an older man named Hamid. "It was so sad."

"That's nice," said Laylee distractedly, fumbling for the latch that hooked the crowbar onto her tool belt.

Roksana stretched and spun as fractured rays of sunlight added a bit of glitter to her gauziness. "What about you?" she said. "*Khodet chetori, azizam?*" Roksana was always mixing languages when she spoke, never remembering to stick to just one.

"I'm fine, too," Laylee lied as she marched forward in the sludge. She stopped to shade her eyes against the sunlight and peered into the distance. Her coffins were stacked in tall, precarious piles, and she still had to get the bodies in, nail them shut, and bury them underground. "Anyway, sorry, guys, I've got a lot of work to do today, so I better get back to—"

The ghosts groaned.

"You always have a lot of work to do!" said Deen, a dead boy about her age.

"Yes, yes, and I'm so sad," said a large, heavyset older gentleman. "I'd very much like to tell you about it."

"*Komak nadari?*" asked Roksana. "Hmmm? Why don't you ever have help? *Baba't kojast?* Who were those kids here last night? Can't they help?"

Roksana was always asking her the hard questions. She was young when she died—still in her mid-forties—but as ghosts went, she was the oldest here; Roksana had been with Laylee just shy of three months now, and not only did that make her the natural leader of their ghost troupe, but it made it so Roksana harbored a special affection for the little mordeshoor. This affection was fairly uncharacteristic of the spirit species—ghosts were usually very grim, you see—but Roksana had a buoyancy that even death hadn't managed to cure.

Anyhow, Laylee was heaving half-thawed bodies into open caskets and just about to answer Roksana's question when three more ghosts appeared.

"Hi, Laylee."

"Hiiiii, Laylee."

"Hey, Layl."

"Hello," said Laylee with another sigh. She sat down in the slush and pulled a coffin into her lap, counting dead fingers and toes. Satisfied, she shoved the wooden box back onto the snow, plucked a business card from her belt, and tucked one end of the triangular card into the soggy mouth of the corpse.

THIS BODY WAS
WASHED AND PACKAGED
FOR THE OTHERWHERE
BY LAYLEE LAYLA FENJOON

"You look tired," said Deen. "It's really not fair that you have to do this all alone."

"I'd help you if I could, *azizam*," said Roksana. "You know we all would."

Laylee smiled as she pulled herself up to her knees. She had an important relationship with her ghosts, but it was a curious one, too; Laylee often felt like their mother, doing her best to keep them in line as they arrived and departed, always afraid for the day they got too bored and did something regrettable to the living. Normally she'd make more of an effort to keep their spirits low, but today Laylee was simply too exhausted to do more than address their most basic concerns.

There was so much work left to do.

Laylee struggled to keep her head up as she moved, pushing through a mental fog so thick she could scarcely remember the steps she'd left undone. It took a great deal of effort, but eventually all fifteen clean corpses were lying in their coffins, business cards tucked between their lips, and now she was nearly ready to nail tops and bottoms together. Laylee allowed herself a quick sigh before reaching for her pliers.

"Oh, *gross*," said Shireen, one of the older girls. "I hate this part. It's so, so gross, Laylee, *ew*."

"Close your eyes," said Laylee patiently. "You don't always have to watch."

And with an efficient, practiced hand, Laylee spent the next several minutes pulling all the fingernails and toenails off her corpses. Once done, she added the human claws to the ever-growing collection she carried in a copper box on her belt. She gave the closed box a firm, swift shake, and then popped the lid, closed her eyes, and chose six nails at random. This was a key step in the burial process, as human nails were the only kinds of nails that would keep a coffin permanently closed.

Laylee unhooked the brass mallet from her tool belt and, hands still trembling, carefully hammered dirty fingernails into the wood. She was grateful that her limbs had temporarily ceased their more vigorous shaking; the larger tremors came in waves, she was realizing, and she was happy to take advantage of the respite now.

Once all the lids had been properly nailed shut, Laylee unsheathed her branding iron and blew a gentle, warm breath onto the metal; the iron glowed orange in an instant, softly steaming in the crisp air. With a robotic proficiency, she stamped the closed coffins with the mordeshoor seal and then, finally, dragged the hefty wooden boxes into the cemetery where, one by one, she melted them directly into the ground.

This last bit was possibly the most fascinating part of the finishing process, because it involved a simple and simultaneously intricate facet of Laylee's magic. Once the dead were ready to be sent off to the Otherwhere, Laylee knelt before each coffin and gently pressed the cargo into the earth. Once in transit, the bodies were no longer her business.

Except—

Well, there's one more thing.

The very final act of the mordeshoor was the ghosts' favorite part of the process, and they swarmed around her now, eager and proud and grateful, to watch as Laylee did her last bit of magic.

The mordeshoor fell to her knees where the dead had been buried and, for each person gone, she summoned a red rose petal from between her lips. These, she then planted into the ground.

In moments, the petals had broken the earth and blossomed into fully grown flowers. It seemed a simple bit of magic, but the roses planted by a mordeshoor would live forever—surviving even the harshest seasons. And they represented a single, unwavering truth:

That a person had once lived.

Laylee's cemetery was a sad and stunning sea of endless red roses—tens of dozens of thousands of them—that marked the memories of every soul she and her family had touched.

And when she finally fainted backward into the snow—exhausted beyond words, hands and arms silver and trembling beyond recognition—her forty remaining ghosts gathered around her, whispered their words of thanks—and then, well, then they did what they always did when Laylee fell asleep on the job. They called for help from the birds nearby.

Not moments later, a dozen feathered friends swooped down, caught Laylee's clothes in their talons, and carried her back to the castle.

Laylee woke up with a start.

The sun had moved a little to the right and snow had descended upon the hills in huge, thin flakes. Laylee was sitting slumped outside her castle door, and she had no idea how long she'd been asleep. Gone already were the earlier rays of warmth, and as she stifled the impulse to shiver, she realized she'd lost another hour of the day.

She staggered to her feet.

There were still forty corpses in her shed, and Laylee would have to hurry up and find Alice and Oliver before it was too late. She had no idea how far the pair had gone or how long it would take her to find them, but she was certain she'd have to leave her property in order to do so.

But leaving home meant she had to bring her bones.

Every mordeshoor was born with two skeletons: one they wore under their skin, and another they wore on their back. It was a symbol of their dual life and the death they carried. The spare skeleton was carefully stacked and bundled into a ceremonial sack where the bones would grow and age just as the mordeshoor did; the second skeleton was as much a part of their body as was their nose, and they could never leave home without it.

Laylee hurried inside to retrieve them, leaving behind her heavy helmet as she did. Once she'd hoisted the bone-sack over her dented shoulders, she pulled her scarlet hood up over her head and drew in a deep breath. With every step she took, the steady *cloc cloc* of clattering bones would alert the world to who she was.

I FEAR
THIS WON'T
END WELL

For all her careful planning, Laylee didn't
need to go far to find what she was looking for. She heard
voices almost as soon as she approached the main road, and
all she had to do was follow the sounds until she came directly
upon them. Alice and Oliver were sitting on their bottoms in
the snow—which would have been curious enough—but more
curious still: they were not, in fact, alone.

Laylee was stunned.

She hadn't actually expected Alice and Oliver to bemoan her
absence, but she was still surprised to find they'd moved on so
quickly. And of all people in Whichwood they should move on
with, it had to be Benyamin Felankasak.

Laylee didn't actually hate Benyamin, but she was feeling territorial at the moment, so she *fancied* she hated him.
When she was feeling more charitable she would tell anyone
that Benyamin was a nice enough boy; in fact, he was her only
neighbor on the peninsula, and she'd grown up going to school
with him. But she'd always thought him a dumb, hapless sort

of young person who spoke with an optimism about life that assured her only of his naiveté. She found his excessive smiles and eager friendliness repugnant, and she couldn't understand how anyone else could feel differently.

Regardless: Alice, Oliver, and Benyamin were engaged in— what appeared to be—a diverting conversation, and Laylee frowned, her eyebrows furrowing, as she felt the familiar pinpricks of envy. It wasn't a fair reaction, as Benyamin was a boy with his own long list of troubles; and though she shouldn't have begrudged him this unexpected kindness of strangers, she couldn't, at present, remember how to be generous. Instead, she was frozen in place, her eyes burning holes into the head of Benyamin Felankasak, when Benyamin—standing some dozens of feet away—finally looked up, evidently aware of her gaze.

He jumped half a foot in the air.

Laylee cut a formidable figure standing in the snow, and Benyamin was right to be startled. She was a vision in scarlet: her long, heavy robes a stark contrast to the pure white of the drift piled up around her. She was livid, hooded, and, in the time it took Alice and Oliver to turn around, storming toward them, her cloak billowing like a curtain of blood in the wind.

Once she was close enough to see their faces, Laylee was beset by a twinge of remorse. Gone in an instant were their smiles and happy conversations; no, now Alice was panicked, Oliver was pale, and Benyamin was bolted to the ground.

Laylee greeted her peers with an insouciant nod of her head and even managed to shrug back a flush of mortification when Benyamin looked directly into her eyes. (Benyamin, you see, was the only person present who knew her eyes were not supposed to be gray.)

Laylee looked away and quickly tugged her hood forward, further concealing her eyes in its shadow, but she couldn't undo what he'd seen. He was still staring at her when she next lifted her head, but his gaze was no longer fearful. His eyes were now soft and sad, and though his pity was somehow infinitely worse, Laylee couldn't help but feel a sincerity in his sympathy, and she knew then that he would protect her secret.

So she touched her forehead and nodded.

Benyamin closed his eyes, touched the back of his hand to his own forehead, and bowed.

It was the ultimate gesture of respect.

Alice and Oliver had no way of knowing what had just transpired between Laylee and Benyamin, but Laylee had at least stopped scowling, which Alice took to mean that things couldn't have gone too badly. This was all the assurance she and Oliver needed in order to get back to the business of things that concerned them:

"Right, good then," said Oliver, directing his words toward Laylee. "I'm glad to see you're feeling better."

Laylee stared at him and said nothing.

Oliver cleared his throat. "You are—feeling better? Aren't you?"

Laylee resisted the impulse to roll her eyes.

Now that she was back among the living, Laylee found she vastly preferred the company of her dead. She couldn't believe she was going to ask these people for help.

"I'm fine," she said coldly.

And then, remembering that it was in her best interest to

finally stop hating everyone, she cleared her throat and said, with great difficulty, "I mean—I meant to apologize . . . for running off like that earlier. It was . . . I may have overreacted."

Silence.

Then, all at once—

"Not at all," said Oliver, who was inexplicably pink around the ears. "It was—yes—it was a very difficult evening—"

"Of course!" cried Alice, all smiles. "And we're just—oh, it's so good to have you back!"

Laylee leveled a dark look at her.

Alice flushed crimson.

Laylee winced and looked away, forgetting again to be nice to the strange children. Laylee needed something from them now, and she knew they might not follow her back to her corpses if she didn't learn to at least *pretend* to be kind.

"In any case," said Oliver brightly, "we were just about to head into town. Would you care to join us?"

Laylee raised her eyebrows, stunned, and turned her gaze on Benyamin; the insect-boy smiled as if to endorse Oliver's invitation, but Laylee shook her head. She cast a careful look in Alice and Oliver's direction and said, "What exactly have they told you?" She was talking only to Benyamin now. "Do you know yet why they're here?"

"Oh yes," said Benyamin, whose eyes seemed to glitter with

barely restrained delight. "Such an odd pair, aren't they? They said they were from Ferenwood. That they'd come all the way here just to help you wash your dead." Benyamin tilted his head. "In fact, Alice was just telling me all about your evening's escapades."

Laylee felt her frozen shoulders thaw. Surprise unclenched her face. And when she next looked Alice in the eye, she said, with great urgency, "Why would you confide such things to a stranger?"

Alice felt her fingers twitch; she wasn't sure, but she felt that this had to be a trick question. Benyamin was one of the most interesting strangers she'd ever met, and besides, he seemed plenty trustworthy. But the mordeshoor was still waiting for an answer. She was looking expectantly at Alice, and Alice faltered.

"Well," she said finally. "It was the truth, wasn't it?"

"But why risk your safety for the truth?"

"*Safety?* What do y—"

"You know nothing of this land or its people or what your confessions could cost you!" Laylee cried. "The people of Whichwood," she said darkly, "are not to be trusted."

"And whyever not?"

"Never mind why not."

"Begging your pardon," Benyamin interrupted. "But I think

I can speak for myself when I say that I'm perfectly capable of being trusted."

Laylee clenched her jaw. "Well, we shall see," she said. "Won't we?"

Oliver clapped his hands together. "Well!" he said, a touch too loudly. "Now that's over with—shall we all head into town, then? Mmm?"

"No." Laylee looked him in the eye. "You and your pale friend said you would help me"—she glanced at Alice—"and now I'm here, asking for your help. I have forty more dead that need washing, and I will require your assistance as soon as possible."

Oliver blinked.

Alice's mouth fell open.

Benyamin was leaning against his wheelbarrow, watching the scene unfold with great interest.

"Well?" said Laylee, irritated. "What's the problem?"

Alice was the first to speak. "You have—you have *forty* more dead people to wash? *Forty* more corpses to clean?"

Laylee felt a knot form in her throat. She hadn't imagined that they would turn her away.

"And we have to wash them all today?" Oliver said, with whispered horror. "All forty of them?"

Laylee felt something inside of her break. "Forget I asked," she said, stumbling backward. "Never mind. I'll be fine. You—you offered, so I—I thought—but never mind. I'd better get back to work. Good-bye."

Oliver caught her arm as she turned to leave.

"Please," he said earnestly. "Don't misunderstand me. We're happy to help. But is there any chance we might be able to take a small break before we dive back in?"

"A break?" Laylee blinked.

"Yes," said Oliver. He tried to suppress a smile and failed. "You know—perhaps we could eat lunch? Or take a bath? Or maybe find ourselves a fresh set of clothes—"

"I don't take breaks."

"Oh, for heaven's sake," said Benyamin, who laughed aloud. He looked at Laylee out of the corner of his eye. "Of all the days to start, let it be tonight! The festivities for Yalda begin this evening, and they're sure to be spectacular."

Yalda.

Laylee had nearly forgotten.

"I vote we take our new friends into town and enjoy the evening for a bit," said Benyamin.

"That sounds wonderful!" cried Alice. "I'd really—"

"No," said Laylee, eyes wild. "No, I can't. I have to get back to work—"

"Your work can't wait a few hours?" This, from Oliver.

Laylee's lips parted in confusion. "No," she said, but for the first time, she didn't seem sure. *A few hours?* Could she possibly spare a few hours? Oh, her bones were so tired.

"How about this," said Benyamin. "If you come into town with us—and enjoy the festivities for a bit—I will personally accompany you back to the castle and lend a hand with the washing. Then you'll have *three* extra helpers." He smiled. "How does that sound?"

Laylee was of two minds. The weathered, beaten mordeshoor within her was at war with the thirteen-year-old girl who still lived in her heart. She wanted desperately to be normal—to have friends with whom she might attend a local celebration—but she could not loose herself from the business to which she'd been bolted.

Still.

The promise of a third helper was more than she could resist. And so, slowly—reluctantly—she relented.

"I'm thrilled to hear it!" Oliver threw an eager arm around Laylee's shoulder (which she quickly shoved off) and said, "Because while I see *you've* had a nice long bath and a fresh change of clothes, we"—he motioned to himself and Alice— "are crawling with filth and, quite frankly, if I don't do something about it soon I'm going to rip these clothes off right here and now, and then, I reckon, you'll all be sorry."

Alice laughed and nodded in eager agreement, and Benyamin smiled at Alice like she spun stars for a living, and Oliver yanked off a dirty sock and flung it over his head, and Laylee—

Laylee was so abruptly and unexpectedly entertained that, for the first time in a long time, she had only to pretend *a little* to be kind. It had been too many years since she'd spoken to so many persons at once, and she could hardly believe she still knew how to do it. Her arms were decaying, her vision was graying, her hair had lost its luster and her bones were bent in all the wrong places and somehow, even now, Laylee had never been more relieved to be alive.

Another small shoot of hope had shoved through the cracks in her heart, and the sudden rush of feeling had left her a little light-headed—and a little reckless. And so she postponed her washing (despite her better judgment) for later, and instead accepted an invitation to go into town and have a bit of fun with children her own age. It was a decadence she'd dispensed with long ago, and its lure was too much to deny any longer.

Just a few hours, she promised herself.

After all, it was Yalda—the greatest celebration of the year— and Laylee wouldn't mind eating one last pomegranate before she died.

The train station was a many-roofed magenta house, bezel-set with hundreds of octagonal windows. It was a wooden relic that had aged gracefully with the seasons, and its ornate wood panels and intricate moldings made it clear that great cost and care had once built this small center of transport. It stood strong and dusky in the snow—determined to creak with dignity as the wind shook its ancient beams—while skeleton trees stood tall on every side, bare branches hung with fresh icicles and hooting owls. As for the train itself, it would be arriving shortly.

The children marched toward the station, Alice's heart racing, Oliver's teeth chattering, Laylee's bones clicking, and Benyamin's brow furrowing as he wheeled his barrow up the slight incline. The massive golden doors opened at their approach, and the four children hurried inside to take refuge from the cold.

✦

Laylee was still adjusting to human company.

The experience was not altogether unpleasant, but currently she felt as though she'd grown three unwanted limbs and hadn't yet learned how to manage them. Alice, Oliver, and even Benyamin (who understood that, for the moment, it would be best to defer to Laylee on all things) looked to her for their every need and question, and she was feeling both flattered and revolted by their attentions. Just now, she hadn't even a moment to dust off her cloak before Alice was touching her and asking whether she might have time to use the bathroom before the train arrived. It was an innocent inquiry, but it was quite a lot to ask of Laylee, who'd spent the last two years of her life in near-perfect isolation. She felt unqualified to answer such a question. How could *she* be expected to speculate on the bathroom habits of another person?

Benyamin was kind enough to shuffle Alice away before any harm was done, but that meant Oliver was suddenly left alone with Laylee, and for long enough to make the both of them uncomfortable.

They took their seats at one of the many long pews stretching the length of the station, and Laylee was finally able to unburden herself of her bones. She dropped the heavy sack onto the space next to her, and the disturbing sounds of a dismantled skeleton echoed throughout the building.

"So," said Oliver, clearing his throat. "What's, um, what's in the bag?"

Laylee, who had not been looking at Oliver, made a great show of turning in her seat. She pulled back her hood and leveled him with a careful, probing stare—a stare so unsettling that he abruptly stood, promptly fell over, and quickly stumbled to his feet. He was breathing heavily as he stalked off, mumbling something about *excuse me* and *beg your pardon* and needing to speak with Alice straightaway.

Laylee covered her face with one hand and smiled.

She was beginning to like Oliver.

✦

The train station was entirely empty save their four-person party and the one lady working behind the ticket window. The lady's name was Sana Suleiman, and she'd worked the ticket window for as long as Laylee could remember. But Sana did not live on the peninsula with Laylee and Benyamin, and more important, she hated her job. She thought Laylee was terrifying and Benyamin horrifying, and though she'd asked management—on at least seventeen different occasions—to have her transferred to another station, all of her requests were met with silence.

(A quick note here: Train tickets didn't cost money.

Transportation in Whichwood was considered a public service and was therefore subsidized by the town; the tickets were just for keeping track of things.)

Laylee walked up to the ticket window just as Sana was chewing on a sizable chunk of her own hair. Alarmed, Sana spat the hair from her mouth, sprang to attention, and spoke without ever meeting Laylee's gaze.

"Hello my name is Sana, and I'll be your ticket master today. It's our business here at the Whichwood train station, Peninsula division, to make your travel dreams come true. May I interest you in a dream come true today?"

Laylee, who'd not only known Sana all her life but, more critically, knew they had only ten minutes before their train arrived (as it arrived every two hours on the hour), was even more curt than usual.

"Four tickets into town, please," was all she said.

But four tickets was three more than usual, and this was an anomaly Sana could not ignore. She turned to look Laylee in the eye for the first time in over two years and stared, unblinking, for five solid seconds.

Laylee tapped the window with a gloved finger and spoke again. "Four tickets, Sana."

Sana jumped, remembering herself, and nodded several times before ducking out of sight. She reemerged with four silky green tickets (which she slid through a slot in the window), and in a strange, uncomfortably sincere voice she said, "Is there anything else I might help you with today?"

Laylee narrowed her eyes, scooped up her tickets, and walked away.

✦

Alice, Oliver, and Benyamin had regrouped.

They were huddled over Benyamin's barrow of saffron flowers; Alice was prodding one of the purple blooms with her finger while Oliver spoke quickly and quietly under his breath. Benyamin was frowning as he listened, and he was just about to respond when Laylee approached. Seeing her, he forced a cheerful smile and changed the subject.

"Anyway," he said loudly, "we'll get the two of you cleaned up straightaway and then we'll see about getting you some proper winter clothes, won't we?" He smiled at Laylee. "What do you say? Don't you think we can set them up nicely? They'll need a good pair of boots at the very least."

But it was Alice who responded. She was pointing solemnly at Benyamin's bare feet when she said, "You mark my words, Benyamin: If anyone is getting a new pair of boots today, it's going to be you."

Benyamin blushed to the roots of his hair. He was both touched and mortified, and he hadn't the faintest idea how to respond. Instead, he stared—and quite a bit too much.

At Alice, that is.

They were awkward, stupid stares, clumsy stares that only grew in number as the seconds ticked by. Too soon, Alice was angry beyond words. In fact, she was horrified.

Alice had had a lifetime of experience dealing with people who stared at her for too long. She'd always known she looked different from everyone else; she knew her extreme paleness often scared and confused people, and it made them cruel to her. But after struggling for so long with accepting her differences, she'd vowed to never again allow anyone to make her feel bad about who she was or what she looked like. Not ever. She had too much pride to waste her patience on the ignorance of insensitive people.

Remembering this now, she glared at Benyamin and turned away. She'd thought Benyamin was a nice enough person; she'd thought he had a trustworthy face and a pleasant demeanor, and she'd felt comfortable with him right away. But now she was sorry for having exercised such poor judgment.

Oliver, who was still lost in thought over their group's brief, heated discussion, had looked up just long enough to make sense of the tension contracting before him now. He was, as I mentioned some pages ago, a sharp fourteen-year-old boy, and he was fully wise to the look in Benyamin's eye. And now, understanding their silent exchange, he couldn't help but be stunned by what he saw.

Oliver had never seen anyone take a romantic interest in Alice before. And though he'd occasionally wondered what that sort of thing might be like—ultimately, the thought of Alice as anything but a friend made as much sense to him as wearing a sweater to go swimming.

(His loss. I think Alice is lovely.)

In any case, things had gone suddenly quiet, and Laylee couldn't understand why. She'd only just rejoined them, and already no one was speaking. Alice was frowning at the floor, arms crossed against her chest, Benyamin was looking suddenly stunned and bewildered, and Oliver, who'd taken all of thirty seconds to stop caring about Alice and Benyamin, was once again so lost in thought about a difficult truth he'd recently uncovered that he could focus on nothing else.

Laylee, meanwhile, had been duly ignored.

Realizing this, the young mordeshoor chose that moment to pass out the train tickets—hoping the gesture would inspire new conversation—but their earlier camaraderie would not be revived. In any other situation, Laylee wouldn't have minded (as she had no great passion for casual conversation), but there was something about her presence that appeared to instill a quiet terror in the others, and she wondered then if *she* was the problem—if, in fact, they simply wouldn't speak comfortably in *her* company. And Laylee was surprised to find that this bothered her.

Which made her a bit mean.

"I'm not your *mother*," she said sharply, apropos of nothing. "You may carry on talking about whatever it is you normally talk about without worrying I'll disapprove."

But just then came the sound of a loud, joyous whistle, and Alice, Oliver, and Benyamin were saved the trouble of having to respond. Bells rang out across the station, and the rush and rumble of frenzy (that always precedes the arrival of a train) sent their hearts into motion. This was it—this was their cue. Benyamin took hold of his barrow, Laylee shouldered her bones, Oliver took Alice's hand, and the four of them charged out the doors and into the cold toward an evening they could never undo.

The train was alarmingly familiar.

Alice and Oliver had arrived in Whichwood on a remarkably similar contraption; the only difference, of course, was that their transport had traveled underwater.

The iteration before them appeared to be an endless string of pentagonal prisms built entirely of glass panels and held together with brass hinges. Each prism was connected by yet more brass hinges, and the lot of them were set upon enormous brass wheels that sat firmly upon the tracks built into the ground. It seemed like a modern, reliable version of the ancient apparatus they'd arrived in—which inspired only a little bit of confidence in our wary travelers—and, sadly, that would have to be enough. Alice and Oliver cringed and shrugged (and hoped these glass carriages would not shatter) as they followed Laylee and Benyamin in their search for empty seats.

The train had pulled into their peninsula station after having already stopped to take on passengers at several other stations, so it was with only a few minutes to spare that Benyamin managed to find two open carriages. He and his barrow took up just over half the space of one, so he clambered in and offered to ride alone. But Oliver and Alice exchanged a meaningful look and, a moment later, announced they would be splitting up: Alice would ride with Benyamin, and Oliver would ride with Laylee. It was a curious arrangement—one that would require an explanation that was yet to come—but there wasn't time to deliberate. Laylee was perplexed and Benyamin was (quietly) thrilled and too soon Alice and Oliver had said their friendly good-byes and the four children took their seats—and settled in for the long ride into town.

It was a beautiful day, even in the cold.

The scenes through the window seemed manufactured from fairy tales: Snow fell fast on curlicued boughs, golden sunlight glimmered across rolling white fields, birds chirped their displeasure at the blustery day, and though it was a fine and strange and dizzying time, it would be the coldest night on record.

Luckily, the glass prisms were lined with plush velvet chairs and a magic that flooded their interiors with a cozy, toasty warmth. Oliver had just taken his seat across from Laylee as the carriage gave its first jolt forward, and she found she could not look at him as she set down her bones. She was not ignoring him—no, she was beyond that now—but there was something about him that felt suddenly different, and whatever it was, it made her nervous. *Would he use his persuasion on her?* she wondered. *Would he try to magic her into a dangerous situation?* More troubling still: She knew he'd *chosen* to sit with her—that in fact he was eager for the privacy—and now that she was about to find out why, she wasn't sure she wanted to.

But Oliver wouldn't be the first to speak.

Finally, Laylee forced herself to look at him, feeling shy for the first time in years. Her irises were more silver than usual today—feverish and bright with feeling.

Still, Oliver wouldn't say a word.

Instead, he leaned forward on his elbows and gazed into her eyes with a seriousness she wasn't expecting. Oh, there was something astonishing in the power of solemnity! Oliver, in his intense preoccupation, was transformed in look and demeanor; he appeared more severe now than Laylee had ever seen him and somehow, simultaneously, more tender than she knew he could be. This transformation suited him (and appealed to *her*) in a way that was rather inconvenient, given the circumstances, but there was no helping the situation: There was a great and quiet dignity in the face of a compassionate person, and not only did this side of Oliver surprise Laylee—it scared her.

Something was terribly wrong.

"What is it?" she finally said. "What's happened?"

Oliver looked up, away, pressed his fist to his lips; only when he'd closed his eyes, dropped his hand, and lowered his voice did he say—very, very calmly—

"Please tell me why you think you're going to die."

It was turning out to be a brisk, frenetic winter day. Diagonal hail had crossed with horizontal snow, fading sunlight slanted through frost sleeping on slender branches, and the fresh, rushing roar of half-frozen waterfalls rumbled in the distance. The afternoon was gently melting into evening and in an effort to change the hour, the sun had stepped down to let the moon slip by. Reindeer peered out from behind tree trunks; black stallions emerged, galloping cheerfully alongside the train; and snowcapped mountains sat still and solemn in the distance, reigning over tall and small with quiet thunder.

And yet—

It was impossibly quiet in the little glass coach.

The wind whispered against the hinges in an attempt at conversation, and still, no one spoke. Laylee touched fingers to trembling lips, terrified to say aloud any word that might collapse her; and though she tried to hide the tremors that shook the tremendous world within her, the bones in the baggage beside her would not quiet their rattle.

Even so, she was not ready to respond.

Of all the things she'd thought Oliver might say to her, this was not one of them, and she was so utterly unprepared for his clairvoyance she hadn't even the wherewithal to perjure herself—or to pretend he was wrong.

No matter: Oliver Newbanks was willing to wait. He was perfectly comfortable on his plush, lavender bench—as the bucolic scenes outside his many windows were unlike any he'd ever witnessed—but the beautiful Whichwood winter could only do so much.

Quietly, he couldn't help but worry.

It was true that Oliver Newbanks was fond of Laylee. Indeed, he liked her as well as any person could like someone they didn't know. There was something about her—something he couldn't quite explain—that kept him coming back to her. It was this same *something* that convinced him beyond anything else that Laylee had no business dying—not now and not ever—and especially not before she'd had a chance to see him as more than just a stranger. Because while it was impossible to identify the chemical magic that fused one heart to another, Oliver Newbanks could not deny that something had happened to him when he first set eyes on Laylee Layla Fenjoon.

He had been marked by a magic he could not see, and it was impossible for him to extricate himself from his emotions.

And here is the strange thing about feeling:

Sometimes it builds slowly, one brick carefully stacked on another over years of dedicated hard labor; once constructed, these foundations become unshakable. But other times it's built recklessly, all at once, on top of you, stacking bricks on your heart and lungs, burying you alive in the process if necessary.

Oliver had only ever known gentle affection.

He had built, bit by bit, every ounce of his fondness for Alice. She was exhausting and frustrating and lovely and wise—she was his best friend in the world. But though Alice had touched his heart, she had never possessed it, and it was this—his racing pulse, his shaking hands, the exciting and disturbing twist in his stomach that felt like sickness—that wrecked and reconstructed him all at once.

Oliver was not simply upset by the revelation that Laylee was going to die; he was deeply and profoundly horrified.

And he knew he could never allow it to happen.

✦

Dear reader: Forgive me. I keep forgetting that you may not have read (or simply might not remember) Alice and Oliver's adventures in *Furthermore,* and I continue to assume you know things you might not. Allow me to explain how Oliver came to know Laylee's secret:

Oliver Newbanks had a very peculiar magical ability.

As I've mentioned earlier, he was a boy generally known for his gift of persuasion. But his talent was layered; in his exploits shaping the minds of others, he'd long ago discovered he was also able to unlock the one thing they kept most confined: their most precious secret of all.

When Oliver first met Laylee, her greatest secret was impossible to decipher. The problem was, Laylee was electric with secrets—her wants and fears were all so equally tangled in secrecy that Oliver had not been able to properly navigate her mind. And though he caught a glimpse of something very wrong when she abruptly collapsed in her yard, it wasn't until she looked him deeply and directly in the eye at the train station that Oliver finally saw her with clarity. Something had changed in Laylee, you see, because she now prized one secret—one fear—above all else, and Oliver was so struck by her unwitting confession he'd run to Alice with the news at once.

They'd shared the information with Benyamin straightaway—as they'd not found a single good reason why this awful news should be kept a secret—and Benyamin, who'd suspected as much after seeing Laylee's graying eyes, quickly shared his own theories. This was what they were discussing when Laylee happened upon them in the train station: The three of them were hatching a plan to help her.

✦

Laylee, meanwhile, had been to war and back, watching the world whirl past her window as she grasped desperately for the anger that kept her safe from difficult and necessary conversations. But this time, the anger would not come. She'd once found protection behind plaster masks of indifference, but she now felt too much and too weak to carry the extra armor. A violent impotence had finally crushed her spirit, and she felt the strength of her resolve dissolve all at once inside her.

Secretly, she was grateful.

The truth was, there was a part of Laylee that was relieved to be found out—to be finally forced to speak of her suffering. She didn't want to die alone, and now perhaps she wouldn't have to.

So she finally turned to face Oliver.

She'd made up her mind to speak as firmly as possible, to emote nothing, and to betray none of the weakness she felt, but he was so visibly shaken—nervous, even—as he looked up to meet her eyes, that Laylee faltered. She'd not expected such sincerity in his gentle, careful gestures, and despite her best efforts to be unmoved, she could not calm her heart. She formed a word and it cracked on her lips. Another, and the sounds fractured into silence. Once more, and her voice feathered into nonsense.

Oliver moved as if to say something, but Laylee shook her head, determined to get the words out on her own.

Finally, her eyes filling fast with tears, she tried to smile.

"I'll be dead by the end of the week," she said. "How on earth did you know?"

It takes exactly ninety minutes by train to get from Laylee's drafty castle to the center of town, and in that time, two separate and important conversations took place in two glass coaches between two sets of persons, hundreds of insects, and one spare skeleton. You already know a bit about one of these conversations; as to the other, I will tell you only this:

Alice, who was not afraid of confrontation, took full advantage of her private time with Benyamin to tell him exactly how she felt about all his staring at her. She made it abundantly clear that she had no interest in being gawked at, and if he had any problems with her, he should sort them out this minute, on account of she wasn't going anywhere and, furthermore, would not apologize for who she was or what she looked like. And then she crossed her arms and looked away, determined to never smile at him again.

Benyamin, as you might imagine, was floored by her suggestion that he thought her anything but perfectly wonderful, and so spent far too long correcting Alice's assumption. In fact, he was so detailed in the many arguments he made to counter the misunderstanding that, by the end of it, Alice had flushed such an extraordinary shade of piglet she worried she'd changed color after all. Horrified, mortified, delighted and surprised— she'd never known she could feel so many things at once.

It was a highly entertaining conversation.

I won't detail the specifics of these separate communications— as it would be an inefficient use of our time to recount the many gasps and glances that punctuate transformative discussions—but suffice it to say that their ninety minutes were spent wisely, carefully, and with great compassion, and that Alice, Oliver, Laylee, and Benyamin disembarked with a lightness of heart that in no way prepared them for the many catastrophes they'd yet to encounter.

And though it would be kinder not to spoil such a moment with the promise of bad tidings, I'm afraid I'll have to stop you here, dear reader, with a warning. These next parts of the story grow terribly dark and disturbing. I'll understand if you have to look away. But if you're willing to venture forth, I must, in the interest of full disclosure, tell you at least this much:

A strange and bloody madness awaits.

BUT FIRST:
A BIT OF FUN
BEFORE THE
BLOOD

Laylee blushed as she and Oliver met the others on the platform. She knew now that everyone was aware of her impending death, and she wasn't sure how to talk around it.

Luckily, she didn't have to.

The thing was, no one but Laylee truly believed the young mordeshoor was going to die. In fact, upon learning of Laylee's unique illness, Alice was quietly relieved. She couldn't be absolutely certain—for that, she'd need to take action—but she thought she might have finally realized what she'd been sent here to do.

And though I've spoken only briefly of Alice's magical talent, I think now might be a good time to say more.

For those readers unaware: Alice Alexis Queensmeadow had the unique and incredible ability to manipulate color. She was born with a pale exterior that belied her vivid interior and, once unleashed, her magic could paint the skies themselves. Even so, she'd never before attempted to color life back into a *person*—but now that she knew more about Laylee's silver eyes and struggles, she wondered whether she had any choice but to try.

Then again, she had to be careful.

Alice had never before used color to revive a person. Her magic had never been manipulated for such serious purposes, and she could see now why the Elders had sent her here—and why they'd assigned her such grave work. They'd suspected better than she what her magic might do, and they'd trusted Alice to have the strength necessary to reinvigorate a person who'd lost what made her whole. For the residents of the many magical lands—Ferenwood, Furthermore, and Whichwood among them—losing color meant losing magic, and losing magic meant the loss of life.

Do you see now, dear reader?

Do you see what Laylee had done?

She'd been depleting her stores of mordeshoor magic with great and unceasing frequency. The illness that overcame her now was a sickness particular to her line of work, which, as an extremely demanding occupation (both physically and emotionally), had finally sapped her of all magical strength. Had Laylee worked slowly, carefully, with breaks and vacations and holidays, she never would've deteriorated to this degree; no, her body would've had time to restore itself—and her repository of magic would've had time to replenish its supply.

But Laylee had not had the luxury of stopping. She'd had no one to intervene on her behalf; no one to share her burden. She was too young and too delicate to have been so thoroughly robbed of the magic still crystallizing within her, and having pushed herself too hard in too short a time, she'd poisoned herself from the inside out.

Alice, who was only now realizing how her magic might be forced to work in this strange new way, was quietly preparing for the task she might be asked to perform. She called upon herself to be steady and brave—but in an honest moment, Alice would admit that the immensity of the task had scared her. This was no small feat, to reinvigorate a dying girl. No, no, this was the kind of painstaking, labored work that would take from *her* as it gave to Laylee; after all, the magic that would save Laylee had to originate somewhere, and Alice would have to use stores of her own spirit to revive the young mordeshoor. These personal reserves would, in theory, help Laylee recover, but Alice would have to make sure she didn't destroy *herself* in the process.

But I digress.

My point here is only to say that Alice was growing more certain by the moment as to why she'd been sent to Whichwood, and she now had hope she might be able to set things right for Laylee. They hadn't had a chance to discuss any of this, of course, as they'd only just stepped off the train, but Alice was eager to put Laylee's fears to rest and make quick work of her duties in Whichwood. (Secretly she was hoping there'd be time left over to enjoy the company of her new friends.) But there was so much to see and do now that they'd reached the center of town that there was hardly a moment to be still, much less to speak. In fact, even if they'd wanted to talk about it, I'm not sure they'd have been able to, as the station was swarming with Whichwoodians toing and froing in the chaos, and Alice and Oliver were struggling to stay afloat. They'd never seen such crowds before—certainly not back home in Ferenwood, where the city as a whole was much smaller—and they were overcome by the madness, grabbing desperately for each other as the masses forced them apart.

Benyamin, like Laylee, wasn't at all surprised by the commotion; in fact, he'd been expecting it. He'd come into town for the express purpose of its busy business (you will remember that Benyamin intended to sell his saffron flowers at the market) and, besides, it was the beginning of *Yalda*, the most important holiday of the year, and people were flooding into town from all distant reaches of the city in order to celebrate.

The festivities were scheduled to begin at sundown—which meant they'd be starting in just a few hours—and Benyamin was hoping to sell his wares swiftly so he might have a chance to experience the evening with his new companions. He wouldn't be able to stay out all night (as was the tradition) because his mother would be up waiting for him, but even a few hours of fun would be more than he'd had in a long while.

Laylee, too, for all her reluctance to celebrate the winter solstice, was feeling inspired to enjoy herself. Her lengthy conversation with Oliver had buoyed her spirits, and the simple reassurance of a sympathetic heart by her side was enough to reinvigorate her courage for just a bit longer. Thinking of Oliver now, she glanced in his direction with an innocent curiosity—only to find that he was already looking at her. Catching her eye, he smiled. It was the kind of smile that lit up his whole face, warmed his violet eyes, and sent a shock of panic through Laylee's heart.

Laylee quickly looked away, horrified, and tried to compose herself.

❖

The four of them pushed and shoved their way through the throng, Benyamin's barrow leading the group. He cut a straight line through the crowds, passersby jumping out of the way just in time to avoid being nicked by his wheel, and the three others followed close behind, sticking together lest they got lost in the shuffle.

The station was abuzz with shouted conversations and shrieking whistles. Diaphanous clouds of smoke hung haphazardly in the air, filtering sunlight in ghostly, gauzy streaks that painted people in binary strokes: light and dark, good and evil. Coats and cloaks swished past in droves; capes and canes kicked up in the breeze; top hats and bowler hats tipped down to bid *adieu*. Pedestrians were bundled in fur coats and boots, ladies were swathed in colorful scarves, children kept warm with mufflers at hand, and babies were swaddled in layers of cashmere. Whichwood was a city of surprisingly stylish residents, whose lace veils and jauntily tilted caps turned the wintertide itself into a fashionable affair.

There were only four persons present whose underwhelming appearance gave the people something to talk about—and Laylee, most of all.

She was impossible to ignore.

Unlike most Whichwoodians, Laylee never smiled; she never said hello, never apologized for bumping into strangers, never spoke at all except with her eyes—terrifying passersby with a single silver look, sharp and inquisitive and alien in the light. Worse: her outmoded attire was smeared in old blood, and her scarlet cloak rippled around her as she moved, whipping open in the wind to reveal the ominous, ancient tools she wore around her waist. It was a disturbing sight, all of it, but even all this might've been overlooked if it weren't for the sound—goodness, the *sound*—that made her so conspicuous. The bones on her back clattered like a second heartbeat—*cloc cloc, cloc cloc*—in an eerie, unworldly echo well-known to the citizens of Whichwood. That sound meant the mordeshoor was among them—which meant death itself was among them—and the people shrank back in fear and horror and disgust. Every bone-rattling step elicited dark looks and pursed lips and hushed whispers. Children gasped and pointed; parents pushed away in a hurry; no one dared interfere with the mordeshoor or her business, but they never treated her with any measure of kindness, either. Even among her own people, Laylee was a pariah, and only her many pretensions could protect her from their cruelty.

Lucky for her pride, Alice and Oliver were too frozen to have noticed any of this.

Cold had penetrated everything, and now that they'd left the warmth of their glass coaches behind, the children were seized anew by the body-clenching chill of the winter day. All four were in a hurry to find shelter, and it was their single focus as they broke free of the busy station. But just as soon as they cleared the crowds and stepped onto the main street, Alice and Oliver were overcome—rooted to the ground in awe and admiration.

In the madness of escaping the station, Alice and Oliver hadn't noticed one very important detail: They were walking on *ice*, not earth. The heart of Whichwood, you see, had few proper streets; it was connected not by land, but by a series of rivers and canals. Summer in the city was navigated almost entirely by boat, and winter in Whichwood—unequivocally the most spectacular time of year—was navigated by horse-drawn sleigh, as the waters froze over so splendidly that they became one continuous, solid surface.

The concrete water underfoot was sixteen shades of blue—waves and bubbles fossilized at their most colorful moments—and the city itself was a sensational old world of majestic domes and terrifying spires, vividly rendered in the still-falling snow. The people of Whichwood were regularly awed and humbled by the magnificence of their own architecture, and Alice and Oliver were no different. Ferenwood was an undoubtedly beautiful city, but it paled in comparison to the grandeur of Laylee's world.

There were more buildings here than Alice could name, more shops, more stalls, more vendors and open-air markets than she'd ever seen. Children ice-skated down the main stretch while merchants shook fists at their recklessness; horse-drawn sleighs carted families from one boutique to another while shopkeepers swept fresh snow into tidy piles. One brave shepherd wove his bleating sheep through the crowds, flurries catching in their wool, stopping only to purchase a cup of tea and candied oranges for the road.

The air was crisp and smelled of cinnamon-mint, and happy sounds could be heard all across the square: grown-ups laughing, children cheering, troubadours marching along with song and sitar. Eager adolescents swarmed glass tubs piled high with sugar-ice candies, raspberries and blueberries and snips of lavender frozen inside each one. Tens of dozens of food carts lined the streets, showcasing towers of steaming beets; endless piles of warm, spiced nuts; tureens of soup and intoxicating stews; hanging ropes of rose-petal nougat; gold platters of buttery halva; ears and ears of freshly grilled corn; sheets of bread larger than front doors; and wheelbarrows stacked tall and wide with hand-plucked pomegranates, quinces, and persimmons.

There were endless sights and sounds to be disoriented by. The city had a heartbeat Alice could dance to, and she was so blown away she was afraid to blink, worried she might miss too much. Alice had been to many strange places in her short life, but even Furthermore, with its infinite towns and frightening oddities, had failed to bewitch her the way Whichwood had. She could only look on, lips parted in wonder, and breathe it all in.

Benyamin and Laylee shared a look of amusement.

"How do you like our city?" asked Benyamin, who made no effort to hide his pride.

Alice, bright-eyed and rosy-cheeked, shook her head and cried, "I've ever seen anything so lovely in all my life!" And then, turning to Oliver, she said, "Goodness, Oliver, what should we do first?"

Oliver laughed, linked his arm in hers, and said, "Whatever we do, can we please do it *after* I've had a bath?"

And this, at least, they could oblige.

Laylee led the way to the nearest *hamam*— the local bathhouse—where the boys and girls would go their separate ways. The many hamams in the city were another public service (which meant they were free for all people in Whichwood), and Laylee had promised Alice and Oliver that the experience would be well worth their time. The bathhouses were famous for their splendor and, stepping inside one now, Alice was able to see why.

The moment she crossed the threshold, Alice was plunged into hot, misty golden light. Clouds of steam pulsed through the open halls, where perfumed towels were stacked on warm racks and robed attendants walked past with pitchers of ice water. Marble walls and floors were interrupted only by pools filled with tempting turquoise depths, and Alice, so frozen only moments ago, thawed instantly, and not seconds later, she was already too warm in all her layers.

Laylee directed her to the changing room, where Alice was surprised to find perspiration beading at her brow. She quickly discarded her ruined clothes, reaching instead for the robe and slippers in the locker she was assigned and, now happily rid of the excess layers, Alice was finally able to enjoy the aroma of rosewater clinging to the air. She closed her eyes and drew in a deep breath, wondering where to start first, but when she opened her eyes to ask, she was surprised to find that Laylee was still wearing her cloak.

"What's wrong?" said Alice, who was already reaching for her clothes. "Do we have to leave?"

Laylee shook her head and sighed. Slowly, she unclasped her cloak—shrugging it off in the process—and then, even more slowly, she removed her gloves.

There was only low light in the hamam, which made it easier for all ladies present to enjoy their privacy, but even in the dimness Alice couldn't help but gasp at the sight of Laylee's withered hands and arms. She was silver past her elbows, and her limbs, which had been growing weaker by the moment, were now trembling beyond all control.

Laylee, however, would no longer allow her emotions to get the better of her. She clasped her shaking hands behind her back and looked Alice directly in the eye and said, "I know you're aware of this already, but I thought I should tell you myself: I'm going to die soon, and there's nothing to be done about it."

Alice hurried to speak, to contradict her, but Laylee wouldn't allow it.

"I just wanted you to know," Laylee said, now holding up one gray hand, "that you have nothing to be afraid of. My illness is not catching. You are in no danger from me."

"Laylee, please," said Alice, rushing now, "I would nev—"

"No," Laylee cut her off again. "I don't care to discuss it. I just didn't want you to be made uncomfortable in my presence." She hesitated. "Though I would appreciate a little privacy while I change."

Alice jumped up at once. "Of course," she said quickly. "Absolutely." And scurried out of sight.

❖

Alice collapsed against a marble pillar and clasped one hand to her chest, wondering how best to handle this difficult situation. The truth was, she'd been ill prepared for meeting Laylee; Alice was deeply intimidated by the beautiful and terrifying mordeshoor, and she had no idea what to say to the girl to gain her confidence. Alice, who had more in common with Laylee than either of them realized, had spent much of her own childhood far-flung from her people and cast off for her paleness. She'd had only one real friend in recent years, and of all people far and wide, hers had turned out to be a boy.

But Alice had desperately longed for female friendship, and though she found much to admire in Laylee, she wasn't sure the feeling was mutual. She worried that Laylee deeply disliked her, and having failed to gain a good rapport with the girl early on, Alice was now terrified she'd set in motion what would become the inevitable disaster of her single task. Even Oliver (who, let us remember, was not technically allowed to be here) had befriended Laylee—Alice had seen their camaraderie, and she envied it—and it made her feel like more of a failure in every moment. But Alice and Laylee were like two halves of the same day, light and dark converging and diverging, only occasionally existing in the same moment.

Alice would have to wait for an eclipse.

The hamam was a big enough, dim enough space that Alice and Laylee did not see each other again until their baths were done. And though Laylee was secretly relieved, Alice was now more worried than ever. She needed to find new time alone with Laylee—and fast. She hadn't realized Laylee's sickness had progressed so much in such a short period, and she worried what would happen if something wasn't done about it soon.

◈

Baths complete, the four children reunited at the entrance, where Alice and Oliver were feeling brand-new—though slightly uncomfortable—in their still-filthy clothes. The only other necessary thing left to do was to purchase sartorial replacements, and Benyamin took this as his cue to say a brief good-bye, promising to return as soon as he sold off his saffron flowers. No one, not even Alice, noticed as he tucked one of the purple blooms in her pocket, and they all agreed to rendezvous just before sundown in order to enjoy the festivities together.

Laylee, who'd been struggling valiantly against the steady, drumming anxiety that said she had no business having fun when there were bodies to be scrubbed, soldiered on, determined to allow herself these few hours of relaxation before she succumbed to the bleakness that was her whole life. She led Alice and Oliver expertly through the crowds—her subconscious always scanning for Baba's face among the many—and delivered them to a string of her favorite shops on the main road. Laylee, who'd never purchased a single piece of new clothing in all the thirteen years she'd been alive, had always admired these many shops from afar. And she never would have returned to the proprietors whose beautiful wares broke her heart if not for the sake of her new friends. They were truly filthy—embarrassingly so—and helping Alice and Oliver was a gift not only to them, but to all people of Whichwood.

Laylee stood off to the side as they perused the many racks of furs and cloaks, offering opinions only when she was appealed to, and allowed Alice and Oliver to indulge themselves in the finery. She'd no way of knowing that the two of them were using this time to form a plan. They huddled over racks of clothes as Laylee towered over the scene silently and, after Alice had described to Oliver the graying decay of Laylee's limbs in great detail, the two of them whispered in quick, nervous breaths about how best to help her. Ultimately, Alice and Oliver decided the best thing for Laylee would be to keep her away from home for as long as possible. They thought distancing her from her work would be the most efficient therapy—and the best way to begin healing her. It was well-intentioned logic: If Laylee didn't use her magic to wash the dead, she couldn't get any sicker. An interesting theory.

Laylee, meanwhile, thought it was nice to spend time with people who could think of things other than death, but she felt it was impractical, too. She could only fool herself for so long, after all; she felt too acutely that she was wasting time in town, affecting the composure of a carefree character when she knew all too well that the demands of her occupation would never leave her. And the longer she was left alone with her own thoughts, the harder it became to think of anything else—even with the many pleasures of Yalda to delight and distract.

The minutes soon multiplied.

An hour had elapsed, and Laylee—who'd done nothing more than lean against a door frame and occasionally shrug a response—was only dimly aware of Alice asking her what she thought of a hat or coat, or of Oliver frowning in her direction, wondering where she'd gone to in her mind. But Laylee could no longer feign interest in their concerns. She'd now spent a total of three and a half hours (let's not forget that the train ride alone took ninety minutes) doing absolutely nothing productive, the last two hours of which she'd spent taking a second (redundant) bath, followed by this—this—*uselessness*. Every lost minute seemed to injure her, every dip of the sun fortified her anxiety, and the more anxious she became, the more convinced she was of one simple fact:

She was making a huge mistake playing tour guide to these strangers.

The people of Whichwood had friendly re-lationships with the creatures they lived among, and their town legislature oversaw not only human concerns, but those of the animals, too. This included business regulations that allowed Whichwoodians to trade goods and services in exchange for a steady supply of fox, mink, rabbit, and wolf sheddings for use in winter clothes. It was a great coup for the people of Whichwood, and now it was for Alice and Oliver, too, who were fully redecorated for the season.

Their choices had been practical and fashionable all at once, and the final composition of colors and fabrics suited them nicely. Oliver was wearing a traditional fur hat—with flaps to warm his ears, a bright red cashmere scarf, fur-lined gloves, a knee-length overcoat of heavy black wool, thick slate-gray trousers, and shiny black riding boots. He cut an incredibly handsome figure in his new clothes—so much so that passing persons, young and old, slowed to stare as he walked by.

Alice, too, was aglow. Her snow-white hair was wrapped in

a shawl of bright, paisley-print wool; the mix of blues, greens, and reds presented a sharp, flattering contrast to her pale features, making her appear more ethereal than ever. She wore a tall fur cap to secure the scarf in place and fastened a heavy violet cape over a gown of gold silk lined in cashmere. Her ankle boots were artfully made but still sensible, and the saffron flower she'd found in her ruined coat was now tucked safely inside her skirt pocket. She and Oliver made a dashing couple despite their best efforts to blend in, and though Laylee stood sentinel beside them—her red hood hiding her face from view—she said nothing of their new attire. She merely looked them up and down and, understanding they were finally finished shopping, turned on her heel and walked out.

❖

Laylee Layla Fenjoon was no longer present.

At long last she'd detached from the hinge in her head that kept her anchored to the world around her, and now she floated along, apathetic and unhurried, impervious to the attempts of her companions to reengage her emotions.

She was, in a word, dying.

She was really and truly expiring now, and she could feel the transformation happening within her. She could practically hear the illness rampaging her fleshy corridors, snapping nerves and crushing organs underfoot. Her hands shook with impunity; her legs threatened to buckle beneath her. Her motor controls were quickly deteriorating, and though she saw the faces of her companions and heard the sounds of their voices, she'd lost the strength needed to push her words in their direction, and so she'd left her body on autopilot, trusting something else to steer.

Laylee had stood up inside of her skin and crawled into a quiet corner of her mind, taking refuge in the steady thrum of some distant, unknowable hum as she waited, with bated breath, for everything to be over. The pains of death came in intervals: sometimes in crashing waves, other times in gentle whispers. Ancient instinct alone moved Laylee's feet, one in front of the other, as they walked along the icy streets; something somewhere inside of her was remembering to be human despite her best efforts to forget.

She'd thought she had more time than this.

She knew the illness was spreading quickly, but she'd figured she had a few days before it dissolved her completely. Something had happened in the last hour to aggravate her condition, and she wasn't sure what it was. Mental exhaustion? Inescapable frustration? The overwhelming anxiety that inhaled her last reserves of strength? Laylee didn't know the answer, but I do, and I will tell you now: Yes, it was all of those things, but it was something greater than that, too. Laylee was sick in more ways than one; she was undergoing a combined physical and emotional demolition, the consequences of which were simply too much for her young body.

And anyway, it didn't matter now.

Laylee had abandoned completely the idea of hurrying back to her corpses; in fact, she no longer remembered why she'd wanted to return to them in the first place. It was a frozen, hateful place that she called home, where nothing awaited her but the emaciated remains of a decapitated life. She didn't want to die there—not among the dead and the decay.

No, she thought.

She would die *here,* among the living, where someone might catch her body as she fell.

I REALLY
DON'T CARE FOR
THIS PART

Alice and Oliver didn't know what to do.

Something terrible had happened to Laylee—they knew this
much for certain—but what it was they did not know, because
the mordeshoor had ceased to speak. Panicked, they decided
the best thing to do would be to take her home—to return her
to the safety of familiar shelter—but when Alice touched Laylee's arm in hopes of getting her attention, Laylee jerked away,
her hands shaking violently as she attempted to steady herself.
Oliver, alarmed, ran forward to help, but Laylee recoiled again,
feverish and off balance. Alice tried to seek help from passing
strangers, but people yelped and hurried away, faces pulled together in revulsion, too steeped in fear and superstition to help
even a dying mordeshoor.

Alice and Oliver were devastated.

The two friends from Ferenwood had no way of knowing
what Laylee was thinking at that strange and terrifying time.
They could only attempt an assumption: Laylee was sick,

yes—this they already knew—but they did not (and could not) accept that she was dying *now*; not here, not in this moment. But—

What if it was true?

If Laylee was, in fact, dying, how were they going to help her when she was refusing to be helped? How could they save her when she was refusing to be held?

And here, dear reader, was the real complication: Alice and Oliver did not know how to help her because they did not yet understand one critical thing—

Laylee's greatest adversary was herself.

Alice and Oliver were familiar with sadness and grief, but they were strangers to the kind of suffocating darkness that could corrode a person—the kind of sadness that was a sickness, the heartache that could colonize lungs and collapse bones—*no*, they did not understand this brand of pain, and so it was not their fault for not knowing what to do. But they'd left Laylee to the clutches of her own mind for too long and the mordeshoor, unmoored, was spiraling into despair. The children meant well, they did—but they were out of their depth.

And Laylee, now swallowed whole by the disquiet that had devoured her limb by limb, could not see the worry in their faces or the anxious looks they passed between them. Laylee's heart had been hermetically sealed in a reckless effort to protect it; she saw herself alone and impenetrable, a drifting body drowning at sea, and she allowed herself to sink straight into darkness, blind and unaware of the many arms reaching out to save her.

✦

Alice and Oliver could only hurry her along as best they could.

The sun was nearly setting now, and they were due to meet Benyamin any moment. *Perhaps*, they hoped, he would have a better idea of what needed to be done.

All the wonder of Whichwood that had been so enchanting upon first arrival was now maddening and ridiculous. The crowds were so densely packed that Alice and Oliver could hardly move sideways without stepping on someone, and it was all they could do to push themselves through the throng without losing Laylee in the process. It was getting harder to see clearly from moment to moment; daylight had been decanted into darkness and the smoky, dusky concoction meant only that the icy night air would soon enshroud them. Quickly now, they pressed on from whither they'd come, forging toward the hamam where they'd promised to reunite with Benyamin before dark.

Seeing his friendly face awaiting theirs in all the dimness was a great comfort to the hearts of Alice and Oliver, who were now besieged by worry. Laylee had grown more insensible by the second, now refusing to even look at them, and heaven help them if they touched her. Laylee was a severed bundle of nerves, electric with pain she had no way of expressing. Oliver, who (like the others) could not make sense of what had happened to her, was doing all he could to stay upright. He would not allow himself to focus on the collapsing girl beside him, because if he were to dwell on the truth for even a moment, he was certain he would burst into tears. Her death had suddenly and horribly become real for him, and though Oliver did not have the words to explain *why* he felt any kind of responsibility toward the girl, he simply knew he couldn't let it happen.

Alice, meanwhile, had decided to blame herself for the entirety of the situation. Oliver's pain, Laylee's pain—all this was happening, Alice had concluded, because she had failed. It was, after all, *her* responsibility to have helped Laylee (it was, in fact, her sole task), and yet, she had failed, and she didn't know how or why or even what to do to fix it. And when she finally saw Benyamin's kind, gentle face, she merely shook her head, silent tears slipping down her face, and said, "I don't know what I've done."

Benyamin didn't have a chance to answer. At exactly the moment he stepped forward to ask questions and offer words of comfort, the sun disappeared beyond the horizon and the world was sapped of any lingering light.

Yalda had properly begun.

Lanterns set fire to the sky. Orange-milky light poked holes in the blackness, brightness consuming the dim spaces until all was caught in its hazy glow. People and places were smudged silhouettes, edges blurred by firelight. There was a moment of absolute silence before the ground underfoot rumbled fast and deep—a sound so tremendous it thundered through the sky, rising in pitch until the heavens themselves ripped open with a seismic *crack*—and the city was drenched in red.

Millions of tiny pomegranate seeds rained down from the sky, and the people—thousands upon thousands of them—stood still and solemn—cups and jars and pots and buckets raised high above their heads—as the steady drumming sound of raining rubies filled the air. It was a moment of reverence and reflection. No one spoke—not a soul moved—as the snow-covered hills and forevergreen trees were painted scarlet in the night. But the rush of so much bounty sweeping fast and hard across the land made it impossible to hear, and even more impossible to speak.

So Benyamin touched Alice's shoulder in a quiet show of support. Alice took his hand in her left, and Oliver's hand in her right, and the three of them stared up at the sky, silently wishing for a world where the beautiful and the terrible would stop happening at the same time.

It was then—just as the sounds of pomegranate rain had shuddered to a stop, and just as the roaring, cheering crowds had shattered into soft noise—that the world went still in an entirely new way.

Alice and Oliver and Benyamin had just turned to look at Laylee when her glazed eyes suddenly came back into focus. She drew in a sharp breath, stiffened, and said, "Please don't let me fall."

Oliver Newbanks caught Laylee's body, and he would not let her go. He cradled her limp, withered limbs, her head resting against his chest, and he ran, madness and desperation telling him to keep moving or die. With each resounding footfall, Laylee's hood fell back, and her floral scarf slipped—the knot loosening at her neck—as a few rogue locks of hair fell elegantly across her forehead.

Laylee had gone silver to her roots.

Benyamin checked for a pulse as they charged toward the train station—Alice shouting at strangers to move out of their way—and though he struggled to find it, he finally managed to locate a weak, dull beat, and with a great gasp of relief, pronounced the mordeshoor not yet dead. Oliver, who hadn't been able to check his silent tears, felt a sudden shock reinvigorate his heart.

Benyamin was convinced that the best place for Laylee to recover was in the safety of his own home, where they might take care of her overnight. Taking her back to the castle, he reasoned, would make it impossible for them to remain with her; they'd not washed any corpses this evening, and so, could not risk having their skins harvested as they slept.*

Oliver, in a moment of clarity, asked if they shouldn't rush her to a local doctor, but Benyamin shook his head—this was not work for a physician; Laylee needed a *magician* to heal her particular wounds, as she was suffering from a disease that affected mordeshoors only. But all of this was beside the point. Let us remember: No one could do what Alice had been sent to accomplish. There was no doctor, no magician, not Oliver nor Benyamin, who could do the kind of magic Alice could manufacture, and she alone would be responsible for what happened to Laylee. Laylee's fate had been tied to Alice's, and it was her job to save the life of this young mordeshoor. She only hoped she hadn't waited too long.

---

* You might be wondering how Benyamin came to be so suddenly an expert on all things Laylee. But you must remember that he was in the unique position of knowing more about mordeshoors than most people, on account of his being their only neighboring family. No one else in Whichwood knew as much about Laylee's life or her grief, and though Benyamin had guilted himself a great deal for not being more of a friend to her, his blame was poorly placed. Young Benyamin himself had such a long list of worries that it was all he could do to make ends meet and keep his own family alive. (After all, it wasn't choice, but necessity, that dictated he lived next door to the dead.) It was not his fault that Laylee fell ill—no matter his protests to the contrary—and I hope that Benyamin—if he's reading this now—will heed these words and, more important, believe them.

As soon as they arrived at the train station, Benyamin rushed to the ticket window. Alice and Oliver stood by, again checking Laylee's pulse and steadying their hearts, while Benyamin secured their passage for four. Once done, Benyamin located an empty carriage and waved them over. Alice, Oliver, and Laylee (still bundled in his arms) quickly joined him in one of the little glass prisms, where, without the bulk of Benyamin's barrow (which, poor thing, he'd optimistically stowed in a public locker in anticipation of an evening of fun), the four of them were able to settle comfortably; there was just enough room for Oliver to lay down Laylee's body on the velvet bench. Oliver's arms were shaking from the strain of having carried her such a long way, but it was the look on his face, desperate and afraid, that worried Alice most.

Wordlessly, faces full of expectation, Benyamin and Oliver turned to look at Alice. They three had discussed the possibility of this exact situation just hours prior, and it was hard to believe the occasion was already upon them. No one had dared to imagine things would fall apart so horribly in such a short period of time.

No matter.

This was it, the moment Alice had been primed for. It would be an arduous, exhausting job—Laylee's revival would be slow and steady, the kind that might take hours or days, depending entirely on the depth of the wound—and Alice could only hope she would do it right. So she fell to her knees without a word and, drawing in a deep and careful and nervous breath, took the mordeshoor's cold, gray hands in hers and began to push color back into Laylee's body.

❖

Meanwhile, the whole of Whichwood was celebrating in the streets, sharing food and drink and dancing to the songs they found in their hearts. The people had no idea what sensations were still in store for them, or which four children were to blame for their impending troubles. No one—not even Benyamin— knew the desperate state of the dead Laylee had left behind. And though there were three friends who might have cared, they were so preoccupied with saving Laylee's life that they couldn't be bothered to think of saving her corpses, too.

At present, said children clasped hands in a train carriage, the glass windows shimmering in the moonlight, as roaring winter winds shuddered against the doors. Even from their carriage the children could hear the cheers of thousands of happy voices: It was a joyous, rollicking crowd still celebrating life and all its glory—but it was what the children could *not* hear that night that was so important. Back on the peninsula, dear reader, in a shed dark and oft forgot, the spirits of a neglected lot seethed at the injustice of their unremembered deaths.

Laylee had gotten their days wrong, you see.

In fact, her mind had been so lost of late that she'd confused days and months altogether. The truth was that her dead had reached their expiration dates several weeks ago—which meant they could've gone rampaging for human skin several weeks ago. It was only out of respect for Laylee that the spirits had remained amenable. But she'd now been gone both day and night, and her sad souls, feeling fully forgotten (you will remember that a ghost is a terribly sensitive sort of creature), could be obedient no longer. They shook their chains until their shackles broke and trees bent sideways to let the spirits pass. They had big plans for tonight, the specters did; they would howl and rage against the machinations that kept them fettered to their molting, festering skin, and they swore on the graves of those they passed that they'd wear new faces by morning.

The troubles of the evening had only just begun.

Alice had been doing the best she could, but Oliver was not satisfied.

He tried to be gentle—to express himself delicately and with consideration for Alice's feelings—but he wasn't quite able to cut the sting of his words. He didn't understand the processes necessary to saving Laylee in this moment, and he couldn't see the level of concentration and careful effort it took for Alice to help the mordeshoor.

It was a delicate dance, you see, to recover Laylee without Alice expending too much of herself in the process. And reviving Laylee could have other side effects, too. Namely: Alice had to be careful not to leave too much of herself—her own heart, her own spirit—in her fading friend. She tried to explain as much to Oliver, but he was too overcome by emotion to be persuaded to think rationally. Though his respect for Alice encouraged him to be patient, he'd secretly hoped Alice would be able to fix Laylee right away. Instead, to his great dismay, at least half an hour had passed and Laylee looked much the same.

The damage, Alice was realizing, was deep indeed.

Laylee's hands were still gray—though Alice was convinced they were at least a shade brighter than before—despite her careful and gentle infusions of color.

Still! There was no need to panic! Not yet, anyway.

Alice was not giving up on Laylee—not so long as the mordeshoor's heart was still beating—and for the first half of their journey home, Alice's steady, unrelenting perseverance and Laylee's gently kicking heart were the only comforts the friends had to hold on to. Benyamin, who was checking every few minutes for signs of life, celebrated each affirmation with a sigh of relief and a triumphant announcement that her heartbeats were getting stronger.

❖

This was how things went on for a while—Alice working, Oliver worrying, and Benyamin doing his best to deliver good news in the interim—until they were just over an hour into their journey (with thirty minutes to go), and Benyamin abruptly ceased checking Laylee's pulse.

His many-legged friends had been worrying at his ear for some time now, but he'd been doing his best to tune them out, determined to focus on the task at hand. The problem was, his insects often worried about him *too* much—and Benyamin had learned to occasionally disregard their overly protective instincts. Tonight, he suspected they took issue with his recent unusual behavior. (It *was* strange, after all, for Benyamin to be spending so much time with two strangers and a dying girl, and they were right to be concerned.) But he'd no time to address their questions at present, and so he'd relegated their clicking sounds to the back of his mind until, eventually, they subsided altogether.

At first, Benyamin took their silence as a sign of progress. But there was another part of him—much like a parent made suspicious by the unexpected obedience of a child—that suddenly worried if everything was okay.

Reader, it was not.

Benyamin's entomological army had its own lead colonel, a spider by the name of Haftpa. (You met Haftpa just once before—he was the muscular spider who scuttled up Alice's nose.) Some years ago, Haftpa had been involved in a tragic incident involving a house cat who'd intended to eat him outright. Haftpa, who was only a child at the time, fought valiantly for his life and, to everyone's great amazement, tottered away with his dignity and seven of his eight legs. His triumph was spoken of in hushed, reverent tones, and he quickly advanced to become the foremost sentinel in Benyamin's brood of insects. But Haftpa was not only a highly respected spider—he was the most admired, too. He was one of the first creatures to burst forth from Benyamin's flesh, and, unlike the many others who quickly fled to find homes elsewhere, Haftpa stayed behind to become one of Benyamin's first real friends. So when Haftpa scuttled forth for a private moment, Benyamin, so sensitive to the wishes of his colonel, could not deny this request—especially as he began to worry that there was, indeed, something he needed to be worrying about.

Haftpa had heard rumblings.

Several of his friends had built their webs in the hinges of the train, and when Haftpa had stopped in to say hello (as was his habit), he found them with curious stories to tell. In honor of the evening's festivities, the train had been making more stops than usual—and tonight, as they trekked past one neighborhill after another, they'd seen unusual things appear in the moonlight. They'd heard unusual stirrings and sounds.

"What kinds of things?" asked Benyamin quietly, who was attempting to stay calm.

Haftpa lifted one small leg in Laylee's direction, clicking quietly as he did. "They sent a warning to you, friend-Benyamin, to be careful in your dealings with the mordeshoor."

Benyamin felt his stomach heave. "But why?" he whispered, worried Alice and Oliver might overhear. "You don't mean— the spirits—"

Haftpa blinked his eight eyes. "We can't be entirely sure of what's happened, friend-Benyamin, as our kind doesn't speak much with theirs. We do not fear the darkness the way your dead do. I know only this: The spirits have left hallowed ground. They will be looking to harvest skins tonight, and there's little to be done if the mordeshoor dies. Your humans must be warned."

Benyamin was horrified.

He knew Haftpa would not lie to him—that in fact he would do whatever was necessary to protect him—but Benyamin couldn't understand how any of this had come to pass. How had the spirits managed to escape?

Benyamin knew a little of the mordeshoor's business, but he didn't know all of it, and so he had no way of understanding, at the moment, what had transpired to make any of this possible. He did, however, understand that *something* had to be done. And soon.

But when he looked up, taking in Oliver's pale face and Alice's pinched lips—the both of them focused solely on bringing Laylee back to life—Benyamin decided it would be best to wait until they got Laylee to safety before he said anything about what he'd learned. He convinced himself there would be no harm in withholding this information just a little longer. *After all,* he thought, *the spirits must have escaped as a result of a simple misunderstanding.* This was the only explanation that made any sense to him, as Benyamin was still operating under the assumption that Laylee had time left to wash her dead. In fact, the more he said this imagined truth to himself, the more he believed it. Soon, he'd managed to dispel any lingering worries.

You must understand: Spirits had *never,* not in all the history of Whichwood, ever escaped the hallowed ground of a mordeshoor's home. It seemed improbable that anything so horrific would happen now.

In time Benyamin would learn the whole truth.

For the moment, all he could do was worry quietly and support his sudden friends through this difficult time. It seemed a wholly incredible thing to him that he'd met these strangers just several hours ago, as he already felt closer to them than to anyone in Whichwood. They three knew without speaking that they could rely on one another and that, somehow, their lives mattered to one another. It was a gift few people received in their lives. And it was a gift Laylee was unaware she had, too.

❖

As soon as the train pulled into the quiet peninsula station, Oliver lifted Laylee into his arms, stepped off the train, and set off running. Oliver didn't know where he was going, but he moved with such conviction that Alice and Benyamin had to race to overtake him. Benyamin shouted for the others to follow his lead, but only occasional lamps were lit in this abandoned land of Whichwood, and it was too dark to see. Benyamin, who did not have spare magic to light the way, did what he always did when he'd run out of options: He asked his insects for help.

At once a storm of beetles and spiders rushed down his legs and out from under his pants and marched on ahead, proud and determined to get their human-friend (and his friends) to safety. Their swarming, feverish mass was lit only by sporadic lantern, misty moonlight, and fourteen fireflies, and so, in the absence of stronger illumination, the sounds of clicking pincers helped the children navigate by sound. Haftpa stood on Benyamin's shoulder, translating directional cues into his human-friend's ear. It was a slow, careful trek. The main stretch of road leading out of the station was fairly clear of snow, but even the occasional mounds, snapped twigs, and scattered pebbles presented treacherous terrain to the many-legged mass, and they scrambled, struggling with grace over each obstacle as it came.

❖

It was a while before they finally reached the forgotten road that led through hills and valleys of waist-deep snow to the small cottage that was Benyamin's home. Oliver, who carried the heaviest load, did not complain, despite having to lift Laylee above his head in order to keep her from getting caught in the drift. The insects—who knew their guidance would be of no use if they were buried under the flurry—crawled back up Benyamin's legs, where their cold, hard bodies took refuge against his skin. In their stead, the flies and bees and ditzy moths (who'd been sleeping behind his knees) took flight, buzzing forward to join the fourteen fireflies, leading the way with all the confidence of professional docents. Benyamin's bug-friends knew the road home better than even he did, and Alice, who'd been watching closely all this time, was quietly awed by the gentle camaraderie that existed between this strange boy and these small creatures.

Finally, a distant light throbbed in the distance, its brilliance flashing like a beacon in the starless night. The moths fluttered forward with a greater eagerness than even before— dizzy with love for the yellow flame—while the flies and bees buzzed back into place behind Benyamin's knees. The remaining army of bugs, now tucked safely inside Benyamin's clothes, remained deathly still, watching for anything at all that might signal new danger. They would protect Benyamin above all else—and at great danger to themselves—remaining vigilant until dawn to make sure their human-friend came to no harm.

It was only when they walked into Benya-min's humble home that Alice and Oliver realized exactly how humble his life was. His house consisted of only one large room informally divided into several smaller sections (eating, cooking, sleeping, sitting—and of course, a little closet for the toilet), but it was a snug, cozy space, its rustic interior warmed by beautiful wooden beams, whitewashed floors, chunky, roughly hewn rugs, a small stone fireplace (from which hung a large metal kettle), and the many happy lanterns that flooded the room with soft orange light. It smelled like hot chocolate and cardamom and the delicate perfume of saffron. And though the home was sparsely furnished, its few pieces were bright and very, very clean.

This, the cleanliness of it all, was the thing that struck Alice the most. It was a simple space, yes, but it was spectacularly tidy. And though it seemed tight quarters for a family to share, it was clear that capable hands kept it carefully maintained.

Alice and Oliver were hugged by its welcoming walls and they settled in at once—perfectly at home in the house of a stranger.

That is—strangers.

Benyamin, who'd only ever known one parent, lived with his mother, who, at the moment, was propped up in bed, staring at them in fascination and understandable surprise.

Benyamin's mother had been ill for two years, you see, and she'd never, not in all that time, seen Benyamin bring anyone home. But then, he'd never had occasion to. The thing no one knew (not even our unfriendly mordeshoor) was that Benyamin's troubles had begun around the same time as Laylee's. It was a matter of simple, unlucky luck.

One awful winter night, Benyamin's home had been struck by lightning, and the thatched roof caught fire. He and his mother were soundly sleeping, and they would have died in their beds if it hadn't been for Benyamin's insects, who did not abandon their friend, but did their best to awaken the sleeping humans even at great harm to themselves. Still, Benyamin and his mother had awoken too late—they'd inhaled too much smoke and were slowly suffocating, eyes blind and burning in the raging fire. Delirious, they collapsed to the floor.

Many of Benyamin's hard-shelled friends lost their lives that night as they came together to carry Benyamin's and his mother's bodies out of the home. It was through their love and sacrifice that he and his mother were spared, and when Benyamin opened his eyes, he was shocked to find himself warm and unhurt, facedown in the snow. He and his mother should've been devoured by frostbite in the deathly chill of the night, but his bugs had saved his family twice over by burrowing under them and around them, linking together arms and legs to cover their exposed, fragile human skin in their own armor.

Benyamin would never be the same.

His love for his many-legged friends, though always steady, had then become a solid, unshakable thing, and he was so moved by their kindness he wept for days at a time. Their great and unwavering affection for him was a support he hadn't known he needed—and he held fast to their friendship more than ever, especially *then,* at a time he needed it most. You see, he and his mother had survived the fire, yes, but there was still devastation to contend with, and his biggest problems were two:

First: despite their best efforts, Benyamin's mother had been badly burned, and her legs, which had suffered the worst, would need a steady supply of time—and magic—to heal.

And second: their once beautiful home (that his mother had built by hand) had been reduced to a pile of cinders, and from the ashes they would have to rebuild with what little they had left. It was now up to Benyamin to support them both.

✤

So when Benyamin walked inside with his three friends, his mother, who'd been waiting up in bed for her son, was more than a little astounded. Benyamin had never done anything so odd before, and it took quite a lot of explaining in order to account not only for the *presence* of his new friends, but also the fact that two of them were from Ferenwood and that one of them was dying.

His mother (whom he called Madarjoon), was not yet satisfied with his answers. She wanted to know everything:

Where had they met;

how long had they known each other;

who were their parents;

why were their parents okay with them leaving home;

anyway, what were they doing here;

what on earth was a Surrender;

speaking of which, why was Laylee dying;

speaking of Laylee dying, when had he befriended the
    mordeshoor girl;

oh, and why was Alice so pale (at this, Alice blushed and
    Benyamin nearly fainted in embarrassment);

why was the tall boy carrying Laylee;

why hadn't Benyamin purchased a new pair of boots yet
    (and oh, for heaven's sake, if it was because he was

spending all his money on her medicine again, she would just lie down and die, and how would he like *that* as a thank-you);

why had no one bothered to tell her that the mordeshoor was ill in the first place;

how long had the mordeshoor been ill;

how long had Benyamin known about this;

why had Benyamin been withholding information from her;

did he not know that she was a grown woman;

had he confused himself for her mother;

did he remember when she told him *she* was the mother in this relationship;

by the way, where had he left her cane;

and why on earth wouldn't that tall boy put Laylee down?

Benyamin, who was clearly used to this manner of questioning, didn't seem bothered. He patiently answered all of his mother's questions while simultaneously making space for Alice and Oliver to settle in, and then clearing off their kitchen table. Once it was emptied, he covered the table with a fresh bedsheet and gestured to Oliver to finally lay Laylee down.

Alice, who was stunned by the loud, curious woman who was Benyamin's mother, was too terrified to say a word. (She can't remember even saying hello to the lady, though Benyamin claims she did.) Oliver, who was only mildly aware of what was happening, managed nothing more than a solemn hello before collapsing on the floor.

Only when her curiosity was finally sated did Madarjoon leave them be, but even then she would not be entirely silent, and, friends, I can't really blame her. Madarjoon had been a jolly, vivacious woman before the fire injured her legs, and this was the most interesting thing to happen to her in nearly two years. She was a woman who worked hard, loved thoroughly, and had strong opinions about everything, and being bedridden did not suit her at all, not even a little bit. She liked to make it abundantly clear at several points throughout the day that if she'd had any choice in the matter—in fact if anyone had had the decency to ask her opinion on the subject—she'd have elected never to lie down, not ever. (And if this was Providence telling her to take a break from standing up—well, she didn't know what to make of that, because upright was the only way to be.)

Alice, who could not think of a single thing to say to Benyamin or his mother (let us remember she was only thirteen, and not yet wise to the ways of charming a grown-up), decided to instead get back to work. Oliver had been shooting her anguished glances since they'd arrived, and though she tried to settle his nerves with a smile, the gesture seemed to cause him pain. So she quickly took her seat at the kitchen table and reached again for Laylee's cold, gray hand. But just as she was about to start the exhausting work, she felt Benyamin sit down next to her. He and Oliver now flanked her on both sides, and their quiet strength gave her great comfort. So it went, the three of them huddled together, hoping for a miracle.

❖

As the night dragged on, Alice grew ever more weary, and Oliver, though determined to stay awake all night, had begun to fade. There were still many hours to go, and Benyamin's mother, who was watching quietly as these exciting events unfolded before her, was becoming increasingly agitated at her son's lack of hospitality. She snapped at him to put on a pot of tea, and he swiftly obeyed. She then asked the boy to get Alice a cushion to sit on, and he procured one at once. Not a moment later, she snapped at him to throw a log on the fire, and he complied. Fully in her element, she took swift charge of *both* the boys under her roof, and soon Madarjoon procured a cure for Oliver's mournful eyes by ordering him to scrub a stack of dishes. Benyamin, who'd begun watching over Alice's shoulder, was again dispensed with, this time ordered to make a light supper. ("Nothing too salty, boy, or I'll bloat like a balloon," his mother said, rapping her cane against the floor.) And, unless strictly necessary, the two boys were forbidden from interrupting Alice while she worked her magic. Benyamin's mother was soon spinning the night on her little finger, she alone thinking of all the little things they needed to comfort and distract in order to make these hard times more bearable. There would be many dark and disheartening moments on this long Yalda night, but it was the sharp, watchful eye of Benyamin's mother that would keep them focused through it all.

Alice had been sitting with Laylee for nearly two hours when she saw the first real signs of change. The mordeshoor's hand, once silver all over, had now begun to emanate warmth and change color at the tips. Laylee was being revived one knuckle at a time, and now that Alice saw the progress, she could estimate how long it would take—and how much of her it would drain—to bring Laylee back to life, and the approximation was dour.

Still, she was grateful for results. She made a quiet announcement about the changes she saw, and Benyamin clasped her shoulder, his weary eyes overcome with relief. Oliver was overjoyed.

Laylee would not die.

She would not be *alive,* exactly—at least not for a while, but she would not die, not yet, and the news was a great comfort to them all. The night was beginning to look up, and the three friends felt their spirits soar . . . alongside thirty others.

The wind had changed.

Ice cracked up the windows. The lanterns flickered in their shells. What had been a soft, whistling breeze not moments before was transformed into a bellowing howl in mere seconds, bringing with it the strange and terrifying chill of something more than winter cold.

❖

The dead, dear friends, had come knocking.

IT'S ALL
TERRIBLY
EXCITING,
ISN'T IT?

Actually, I should clarify: Ghosts cannot knock. They don't have knuckles or skin (or fleshy bits of any kind), so they're really only good for rattling things, toppling things over, and making loud, frightening noises. They would've *liked* to have knocked, but the simple fact of their being ghosts made those human courtesies impossible. So it was despite their best efforts to be polite that they shook the door off its hinges.

Now, let us take a moment to remember something important: Regular people could not see ghosts. Laylee (and Baba, wherever he was), were the only ones who could see the spirits, so, when the front door had simply fallen out of its frame for (what appeared to be) no apparent reason, Benyamin and his companions had no way of knowing what had happened. Their little heads had popped up, startled and afraid, searching for the culprit and finding none.

The ghosts took great offense to this.

They were tired of being so soundly ignored by man and mordeshoor, and even though they knew better than to expect regular humans to recognize them, they were feeling sensitive as of late, and so took the slight personally. This did not help the situation.

As you might recall, the last we heard of the ghosts was that they'd been angry about Laylee having abandoned them, and that they'd broken free of their shackles and set off at once to see about getting new skins. But you might also remember my mentioning that it was their respect for Laylee that had kept them so obedient in the first place. Well, this was true. And once they'd finally broken free of her hallowed home and begun to roam the earth (a thing no ghosts had done before in all the history of Whichwood), they began to have second thoughts about their plans to steal skins from living humans. After all, the ghosts knew many of these humans—some were their living relatives—and they'd grown a conscience in the last few hours. So they reconvened.

They decided it would be best to try and speak with Laylee first—to figure out what had happened to make her abandon them so completely—and only then, once she'd had a chance to speak with them, would they make their final decision. They had hoped to be reasonable; the mordeshoor had tended to them—perhaps imperfectly—but they knew that she worked alone, and though on occasion they liked to have fun at her expense, they quietly respected the young girl for her unwavering dedication to a thankless occupation. After all, there were many ghosts who *wanted* to cross over to the Otherwhere, and without Laylee, they had no means of doing so.

If they were able to find the mordeshoor—and if her words were convincing enough—they would agree to go back to the castle and have their spirits and dead selves be shipped off to the Otherwhere (with Laylee's assistance) at once. But if her answers were somehow unacceptable, they would have no choice but to spear some flesh and take it as their own, because they were running out of options in the mortal world. They had little time left in the grace period before their spirits would simply disintegrate, and that, of course, was the least favorable outcome of all.

So they'd done their due diligence, searching high and low, on train and terrain to find the young mordeshoor, all to no avail. They were certain she would be at the festivities tonight, and still, they were unable to find her. Frustrated, the last of their patience quickly fraying, they returned to the castle for one last look around, when one of the ghosts, a young boy who'd noticed the light coming from Benyamin's little home, pointed out that the lone cottage was the one place they'd yet to look.

This was how they found themselves, all forty ghostly

bodies, crowded cheek by jowl (figuratively, of course) in the cramped home of Benyamin Felankasak, where they had finally found their mordeshoor. Now, had Laylee been *awake,* she might've been able to tell someone that Benyamin's small home had been infiltrated by a large group of angry ghosts, but as it happened, she was not. And so there was no one at all to explain the sudden drop in temperature or the unexpected departure of the door from its frame.

The humans in Benyamin's home could only wonder at what had happened, and it wasn't until Haftpa spoke quietly in the boy's ear that anyone could understand enough to be afraid.

❖

The ghosts had been waiting around for at least five minutes, shouting their frustrations for anyone to listen (and not understanding why Laylee would not look at them) when Benyamin's sentinel finally offered to act as liaison between the dead and the living.

Animals and insects had no problems interacting with the unseen; they spoke a common language that humans were only occasionally made privy to, as their worlds were run with more order and compassion than ours: Namely, the nonhuman world did not hunt the creatures they feared; they simply stayed away from them. And now, though Haftpa had never had much to discuss with a ghost, he was willing to act as a neutral party in order to facilitate some kind of goodwill.

He quickly recognized the head of the group—a tall, brooding ghost-woman named Roksana—and explained the situation: Laylee was dying; the other children were trying to resuscitate her; they didn't know how long it would be until she woke.

Meanwhile, Benyamin was (hastily) explaining to the humans what had happened.

"What?" This, from Benyamin's mother. "What do you *mean* the ghosts escaped hallowed ground? How is that possible?" she cried, nearly falling out of bed in horror.

"They're here right now?" asked Oliver, who'd gone pale. "In—in here? Right now?"

"What do they want?" said Alice, who'd gotten to her feet. "Are they upset?"

Haftpa reported that, yes, they were very upset. They wanted to know what had happened to their mordeshoor. They wanted to know why she'd left them alone for so long. And they wanted to know whether she would be coming back.

Benyamin hurried to explain exactly what had happened to Laylee, but instead of de-escalating the situation, Benyamin's explanations had apparently made things worse.

Roksana shouted out so angrily in response that Haftpa

jumped up, startled, and spun an unexpected web in the process. She was enraged to hear that the mordeshoor had been left to die like this. The dead were nothing if not soulful creatures, and they felt great pain and pity for the mordeshoor that they, the ghosts, had taken for granted. Laylee had been treated poorly by her people, and now an entire other civilization of beings would suffer as a result. What would happen to the dead once their only remaining mordeshoor died? (*Never mind the crazy father,* said Roksana.) What did the people of Whichwood think would happen? Had they expected that they could just discard this young girl and her position with no care or thought to her well-being? Did they not see the shortsightedness of their own actions?

This thirteen-year-old girl had been left to suffer all alone, with no one in their busy, bustling city stopping long enough to care. The ghosts, understanding this all at once, were no longer simply angry—they were enraged to the point of asphyxiation. Roksana could hardly speak for all her fury. And she and her ghosts huddled around Laylee's body, suddenly sorry for ever having given her a hard time. They knew they could be annoying, jumping out of corners and being occasionally absurd and unkind—but they were desperately bored for conversation, and Laylee was the only human with whom they could interact. She kept their secrets, and helped soothe the pain of passing. She was the only living person to care what happened to her people when they passed on, and the ghosts valued her dedication to them.

So this?

This would never do.

Haftpa had quickly explained Roksana's sudden outburst, and Benyamin, who hurried to carry out the translation to the others, had begun to whisper the words, so terrified was he of what Haftpa had told him. The ghosts had come to find Laylee in hopes of making amends, but now, having discovered the truth of how terribly she'd been treated, they sought to exact revenge.

The ghosts' consciences would be clear tonight.

It was clear to them that by mistreating Laylee, the Which-woodians did not respect the rites and rituals that affected their dead and, family or not, the spirits would not defend those who'd stood silently by as their unseen world was plagued by injustice.

"Wait," cried Benyamin, who was now beseeching the ghosts blindly. "Please—we're doing the best we can to help her—we just don't know how long it will take—"

"We recognize your efforts," said Roksana, and Haftpa hurried to translate. "As a thank-you for your loyalty to the morde-shoor, we will not harm the four of you here tonight. But we will not grant the same protection to the people celebrating in the streets. They dance and feast while their mordeshoor dies!" Roksana cried, shaking her fist. "This, we can never forgive."

In the time it took Haftpa to translate the rest of her message, the ghosts had already gone, charging wrathfully into the night—

Heaven help the humans whose paths they crossed.

"What do we do?" cried Alice, who was look-ing from Laylee to Benyamin to his mother to Oliver and back again. She couldn't possibly abandon Laylee, not now, not at this critical juncture, but it was also true that they couldn't just wait here while the ghosts charged into the city to strip innocent people of their flesh. "What do we *do*?" she said again, when no one responded.

Oliver opened his mouth in an attempt to speak, but no words came out. Benyamin looked to Haftpa for advice, but the little spider wasn't sure what to say. Madarjoon was the only one who didn't seem too stunned to speak. She was shaken, yes, but she hadn't lost her wits, and it was her quiet, adult authority that rang true and clear in their young bones when she said simply, "You must go. At once."

"But what about—" said Alice.

"You must take her, too."

"Take her with us?" said Oliver, eyes wide. "How?"

"Put her on the train and take her with you," said Madarjoon. "You will make it work; you cannot leave the mordeshoor behind. Alice will stay with her, healing her as you go, and hopefully, before the end of the night, she will have been able to help the girl enough to get her eyes open."

"But why?" said Benyamin, who was seeing something in his mother's eyes that only he, her son, could recognize. "Why do we need to take her with us?"

"Because," said Madarjoon, "once her eyes are open, you'll be better able to see what's happening."

"What do you mean?" said Oliver.

"Laylee can see the ghosts," said Madarjoon. "She knows them personally. That much was made clear tonight."

Benyamin blinked, surprised. Oliver didn't know what to say. Alice looked at the unconscious mordeshoor and said, "Yes, it would make sense if she did. Though I wonder why she never said anything about it before."

"Because she's a smart girl," said Madarjoon. "She knows better than to make that kind of information public. It's hard enough being the caretaker of dead bodies; but to have to act as liaison between human and spirit? Can you imagine how many grieving people would harangue her about communicating with the spirits of their loved ones?" Madarjoon shook her head. "No, it's better that she kept it to herself. But the ghosts made it clear tonight that they knew her personally—that they'd talked before, that they cared for her. That sort of relationship cannot come from nothing. Mark my words: That girl can see the dead—and can speak with them, too. And if you're going to have any luck at all tonight, you're going to need her with her eyes open. So go. And hurry. You have no time."

Benyamin checked the clock and said anxiously, "But the trains won't come for another hour—what do we—"

And Madarjoon grabbed for her two canes—resting just to the side of her bed—and pulled herself up, with great effort, to stand on weak and withered legs. She wore a long pink nightgown with a ruffled collar and scalloped hem, her hair tied back with a small silk bandana. At her unexpected movement, Benyamin rushed forward, alarmed, but Madarjoon held up a hand to stop him.

"Come along, children," she said carefully. "Let me do the only kind of magic I'm good for anymore."

"But, Madarjoon," Benyamin cried, running forward, "you're not strong enough—"

She cut him off with her cane. "A piece of advice, sweet son of mine: Never, ever again tell a woman she's not strong enough."

"But I didn't mean—I never—"

"I know." She smiled. "Now come along." She glanced at Oliver and Alice. "All of you."

"Where are we going?" asked Alice, hurrying forward.

"We'll get to that in a minute. Hurry up, hurry up," she said, hobbling forward to prod Oliver with her cane. "Come on, then. We haven't got all night." Oliver jumped up, startled, and reached for Laylee, preparing to lift her into his arms again when Benyamin's mother cried, "Get a barrow, boy! No need to waste time flexing your muscles."

Oliver flushed, embarrassed for a reason he couldn't quite explain, while Benyamin ran off to collect one of the extra wheelbarrows he used for his saffron harvest. The children lined the rough interior with pillows and bedsheets, and then, carefully, settled Laylee inside, taking care to tuck in her bag of bones beside her. Suddenly, for just a second, her eyelids fluttered.

Alice gasped.

The four of them peered in, looking for another sign of life, but this time Laylee was still.

"Everyone's got their coats?" Madarjoon said loudly, looking over the heads of the children. "You've all used the toilet? No? Well, best hold it in. Come on, then—let's carry on."

And they shuffled outside into the cold, biting night and hiked in taut, nervous silence for a matter of at least fifteen minutes, through hills and valleys of thigh-high snow (through which Benyamin had no idea how his mother managed), until they reached the very edge of their quiet peninsula, and could hear the ferocious waves lashing against the cliffs.

Alice and Oliver were just shy of terrified. They had no

interest at all in summoning what was left of their glass elevator, and they had no idea whether that was what Madarjoon had been hoping to find. In fact, they sincerely hoped it wasn't, because if it *was,* they didn't know how they were going to explain to her that they'd broken it.

Luckily, that wasn't at all what Madarjoon was thinking.

She hobbled out to the very precipice, a point nearly invisible in the blackness of night. The children were too afraid to follow her, and when Alice whispered her worries to Benyamin, he assured her that everything would be okay. Madarjoon had, in fact, done this many times before.

There was a reason, you see, why Benyamin had never had to explain his strange relationship with the many-legged world—and it was because his mother never needed an explanation. She, too, had a special relationship with the nonhuman world, and she would call upon that friendship now, at a time she needed it most.

When Madarjoon stepped back from the ledge some moments later, it was only a matter of seconds before the sea—already churning with great and tremendous turbulence—began to lurch ever more tremendously. As the sea rocked back and forth with the dizzying force of a thunderclap, from its tremulous depths came a sudden and unmistakable expulsion of air, and a sound like a blasted rocket—*crack!*—snapped the seas wide open.

A whale as large as a pirate ship bobbed at the surface of the water, its large fin slapping hello to an old friend. Madarjoon spoke quickly and quietly to her comrade, and the children, struck still with awe, stood silently by, waiting only to be told what to do. There was little time to spare, so the formalities were dispensed with. The whale-friend took only a moment to slap its fin in acknowledgment to whatever secret thing Benyamin's mother had said to him and, a moment later, yawned open his mouth to allow them aboard.

Benyamin reassured his stupefied friends that he'd done this before. "It's perfectly safe, I assure you—"

"Come along, children," said Madarjoon. "We've no time to assuage your feelings. There are lives to be saved." She took another step toward the whale, but Benyamin threw out an arm to stop her.

"Are you—I mean," Benyamin stammered, frozen, "are you coming with us?"

"I know you're a little old for my company," said his mother with a smile, "but I'm afraid it's best if I come along for the night, considering the circumstances."

"But are you sure you'll be alright?" he said nervously. "You're not too weak to—"

"What did I say to you about accusing a woman of weakness? Do I look weak to you? I carried your bones *inside* of me, young man. A person doesn't need legs to be strong. I've got enough heart for ten legs, and that'll carry me farther than these limbs ever did."

And without another word, she stepped off the edge of the cliff and fell, with a whistling *whoosh,* right into the open mouth of a humpback whale. Stunned and humbled, Alice and Oliver and Benyamin hastened to follow. They each held on to a different side of the wheelbarrow carrying their friend and, with a nervous intake of breath, took a running leap off the cliff—

And fell softly into the jaws of their sea captain.

As you might have expected, it was not a comfortable journey. In fact, it might be an understatement to say that whales are not ideal for transporting humans. But this whale was doing their group a huge favor, so they would have to make do with what they had. The group didn't speak much as they jostled one another in the wet, sucking maw of the sea creature, as there was little positive to say. Each was lost in his or her own mind, every person thinking thoughts more diverse and interesting than the next—and as the conscious among them stood tall and still in the moist quiet of the whale's mouth, it was all they could do to hold on to one another and hope they'd make it to town before the ghosts did.

But our protagonists would not be successful tonight.

I will tell you this now: It would be impossible to beat the ghosts to town. The spirits had a head start and, even though the whale moved at a tremendous clip under the sea, they would still be deposited at the edge of the open water—certainly closer than before, but still a bit far from the center of town. By the time they clambered out of the whale's mouth and onto hard ground, they would still need to travel another twenty minutes or so by foot before reaching the Yalda celebrations.

It seemed a fruitless effort—with one exception.

Alice had not been idle. She'd been working with the mordeshoor through light and darkness, on land and at sea, pulsing color and magic back into her limp limbs until the little progress she made begat more progress, and soon, the mordeshoor was healing at an exponential rate. She was healing now in much the same way she fell ill: Each milestone was bigger. First a knuckle, then three, then four fingers, then the whole hand; by the time they reached land, Alice had managed to undo the gray as far as Laylee's elbows, and though the mordeshoor was still too weak to stand, she was able at least to flutter open her eyes.

It was, as I've mentioned several times already, a very dark night. This darkness, plus their urgency to shove forward toward the city center, distracted the rest of the group from the miracles being performed beside them. So you might understand why it took a moment before anyone realized that Laylee had opened her eyes.

(Though it was, understandably, Alice who saw her first.)

"Laylee!" she cried, her heart swelling with joy. "You're awake!"

"She's awake?" said Oliver, hardly daring to breathe.

"She's awake!" said Benyamin, who turned to his mother with pride.

"I knew she'd open her eyes in time," said Madarjoon, who was hobbling along as best she could, huffing and puffing and never complaining, grateful to be on her feet again.

Laylee was terribly confused. It took a lot of explaining what had happened to her (and why she was lying in a wheelbarrow as they pushed her through empty midnight streets) before she finally clicked everything together, and when she did, she was stunned.

"You saved my life?" she said to Alice. "But how?"

"It's what I came here for, remember?" said Alice, eyes shining in the moonlight. "I said I'd come to help you. We all did," she added, beaming at her friends (old and new) with great happiness.

"So—you knew?" said Laylee. "You've always known I was going to die?"

Alice shook her head. "I didn't. But someone must've known; otherwise, the Ferenwood Elders wouldn't have sent me here. They must have heard about you from someone in Whichwood. They made a great exception to send me here," Alice explained. "We don't normally travel to other magical lands."

"So strange," said Laylee, who already seemed exhausted.

She let her head rest against the wheelbarrow as Oliver pushed her forward, and said only "so strange" once more, before her eyes closed again.

No matter. They pushed on, their spirits higher than ever; it was a great help to their hearts to know that Laylee was healing—and that, hopefully, she would survive—especially as they charged forward into the endless winter night, desperate to save the people of Whichwood from an untimely end. It was an unlikely group of individuals upon whom depended the salvation of an entire city, but the insect boy, his injured mother, his colorless friend, her curious companion, and the nearly dead girl asleep in the wheelbarrow would have to do. It was, admittedly, hard to imagine them besting a crowd of angry ghosts, but they would at least have to try.

BRACE YOURSELF
BEFORE YOU
READ ON,
I BEG YOU

As I said: They were too late.

It was an admirable effort on their part, charging into the city like they did, but the city was already in chaos when they arrived. Alice, who had been holding Laylee's hand this whole time, was helping the mordeshoor get stronger in every moment. Laylee's eyes occasionally flickered open long enough to retain new information about their situation and, fortified anew, she was ready to guide with her eyes when necessary.

Unluckily, there was little to be done.

The mass of happy people they'd seen swarming the streets just hours before was nowhere to be found. Instead, bloodcurdling screams rang out across the city, parents fainting in the streets while their children sobbed helplessly at their sides. Food stalls had been knocked sideways; lanterns had been shattered on sidewalks; cocktails of blood and pomegranate juice dripped down snowy banks and streets, scarlet tendrils snaking across the land.

Of the forty spirits unleashed upon the city, just under half of them had already unzipped humans from their flesh. That left twenty-two of them wandering about the city, still haunting the remaining humans, taking their time choosing which skin they liked best.

This created two very awful scenes in the street.

First, and perhaps most disturbing: The humans whose skins had been harvested were still alive. They stumbled around, muscle and bone exposed to the elements, bleeding uncontrollably and retching at intervals. They could survive in this condition for no more than an hour, during which time the ghosts who'd stolen their skins were afforded the opportunity to return the skin to its owner. If not, the bloody remains would simply collapse. We could not know exactly how long it had been since their skins were stolen, but it had been at least some many minutes, and time was running out. Worse still: It was horrifying to witness. Eighteen skinless bodies staggered in the ice and snow, slipping repeatedly in pools of their own blood and bile, while their children looked on in horror. Thus far, only adult bodies had been chosen for harvest, as their skins were most roomy.

Which brings us to the second set of awful scenes in the street: The ghosts, who'd eagerly and clumsily pulled on their fresh human flesh, could not understand why they weren't immediately accepted by the rest of the living society. They stumbled around, untroubled and excited to join the others in the night's festivities, and were made only angrier by the full and thorough rejections they received. They finally looked like the others, didn't they? They looked like they used to, didn't they?

The trouble was, the spirits had no access to a mirror; if they had, they might've noticed that the skins they'd stretched over their spirits were bunched up in all the wrong places—and too tight in others. It had been a long time since they'd been human, you see, and they couldn't remember where everything was supposed to go. Their noses were on their foreheads and their lips were where the nose should be; fingers were only half filled, and elbows had gone where shoulders should; one ghost had put his leg into an arm, and another had zipped the whole thing on backward, and—anyway, suffice it to say that they were not as attractive as they'd hoped to be.

So there it was: The beautiful, incomparable streets of Whichwood had gone slippery with the blood of the still-living, who staggered sideways and frontways, scarlet icicles forming along their beating hearts as fresh blood dripped down their vulnerable bodies.

✦

Seeing all this, Benyamin's mother fell to her knees.

She was a strong woman with an iron will, but this was too much even for her to stand. Her legs, already weak from the effort to get her here, could no longer keep her steady, and so she sank to the ground, her mouth unhinged in shock, as the dead skins taunted the stumbling remains, and the whole of Whichwood lost their minds in horror.

Still, there was work to be done.

The children were unusually composed in the face of unspeakable terrors. For Alice and Oliver and Benyamin, the situation felt somehow surreal, intangible, and dreamlike, but for Laylee—well, for Laylee, it was just another day at work.

The mordeshoor, who'd been invigorated enough to speak clearly, asked Alice to unhook the whip hung from her trusty tool belt. Alice quickly complied and, with Laylee's careful permission and instruction, cracked the whip through the air three times.

The spirits—far and wide—stood still.

Alice cracked it thrice more. The vagabond spirits, still susceptible to the methods of the mordeshoor, screamed out in surprise. Once she knew she had their attention, Laylee spoke quietly. Her words were for the spirits alone, and she knew they would hear her.

"Come here," she said softly. "I'd like to speak with you." And she instructed Alice to crack the whip until the ghosts came.

Benyamin, meanwhile, had formed a plan of his own. With enough time, perhaps Laylee could convince the ghosts to give up their human skins, but right now they needed a temporary solution for these quickly deteriorating bodies, and fast. Benyamin spoke quietly and urgently with his creatures, and though no one could've known for sure that Benyamin's plan would work, the insects quickly agreed to help. But this was the kind of plan that would require the assistance of nearly all the many-legged residents of Whichwood, not merely the ones who were loyal to Benyamin. Haftpa set off with his troops at once, promising Benyamin that they would return with as many recruits as possible.

While Haftpa scuttled off in search of more compatriots, Laylee's twenty-two remaining ghosts had begun to gather. It took longer than Laylee would have liked for them to show their faces, but then—well, they were a bit mortified to have been found out like this. The ghosts still felt they'd done right to avenge their mordeshoor, but somehow they knew she wouldn't approve of their methods, and they couldn't bear to face her. Fortunately, they didn't have a choice in the matter. There was a definitive kind of magic that tied the ghosts to her, and they could not disobey her call so long as she was alive. And so they floated cowardly forward until they stood before her, transparent heads hung in shame.

No one but Laylee could see what was happening, but that didn't matter. Her friends stood by apprehensively, ready to step in should she call upon them.

"Do you see now?" Laylee said to her dead. "Do you see

what it would be like to stay behind?" She lifted one weak arm to point at the bumbling skins inhabited by the ghosts pretending to be human, their lopsided arms and noses sending passersby screaming into the night. "They are reviled. They leave in their wake nothing but blood and madness. You," she said to the still-gauzy spirits, "in an unfamiliar flesh, would not be accepted back into your families. You would not be invited back to society. Your time here has come to an end, friends. You have to trust in the hourglass of the worlds," she said. "You must move on when it's time to go."

"But you abandoned us!" cried one of the ghosts. "You left us behind—"

"Never," said Laylee. "I would never. I fell ill only because I tried too hard. But I would never abandon you to this fate," she said, nodding again to the devastating scene before them. "You are my charges in this world, and it is my duty to protect you.

"Please," she said softly. "Let me help you move on."

Haftpa had returned.

The city could *hear* them approach before they saw their small, creeping bodies, thousands upon thousands of hard-shelled creatures charging into the center of town. Benyamin's plan was for the insects to form protective armor around the skinless humans just long enough for Laylee to convince the eighteen ghosts to give said skins back to their human owners. Haftpa scurried forward as quickly as he could, climbed atop Benyamin's shoulder, and receiving the signal from his human-friend, he lifted one leg to unleash his comrades upon the night.

Tragically, they were already too late.

Just as the insects charged forward, four of the skinless bodies collapsed, unmoving, to the ground. The impossible moment was so saturated with madness that there was no time to stop—no time for Laylee to lose her head—no time at all to pause and mourn the four innocent lives they'd been too slow to save. What could she do? How would she answer for this?

Laylee's head was spinning. It was simply unacceptable that anyone had died; improbable that she was not dreaming.

Had she dreamed it?

The sounds of the world seemed to surge back into her consciousness. Suddenly she heard a rushing stream of clicking legs thrusting into the darkness, parting people and places, climbing over upturned wares and shattered lanterns. The mass of bugs poured all at once into the center square where the remaining bloody, skinless human figures were still staggering and, in a moment of horrible necessity, climbed atop the soggy masses of flesh until the still-alive fourteen bleeding human bodies were swallowed up by a sea of sharp black exoskeletons. The thousands of insects moved in choreographed perfection, linking arms and legs in a synchronized procession, clicking into place to create temporary armor. The entire act took no longer than several minutes, but the world seemed to slow in that time, strangers looking on with a combination of awe and revulsion as the entomological world came together to spare these human lives.

The armor would afford them at least a few more hours of protection, and in that time, Laylee and her troop would have to move quickly. Instinct alone was keeping Laylee afloat. She didn't know if anyone else had noticed yet, or if any of her friends had seen what had happened. Alice and Benyamin rushed forward to usher the now-armored bodies away from the awkwardly skinned ghosts; Laylee still needed time to negotiate with the ghostly thieves who'd stolen the human skins, but at least until then the human bodies, now protected from the elements, were able to move with ease and quickly ceased their retching.

Laylee, who was still negotiating with her spirits, was making requests from her wheelbarrow, and Oliver, her newly appointed assistant, was only too happy to oblige. They would have to get everyone back to the castle as soon as possible, and they would need as many volunteers as they could get. They would have to wash forty-four corpses tonight (including the four newly dead bodies), or many more innocent people would die before morning.

✦

Benyamin's mother took it upon herself to gather the volunteers. She promised to go door-to-door, collecting as many helping hands as possible, and would meet them back at the castle. But she urged them not to wait for her.

"Go," she said. "You take the train—it'll be arriving any moment now—and I will meet you at the castle. We'll take transport by water."

So they split up.

Alice, Benyamin, Laylee, and Oliver herded up the ghosts, the armored humans, and the skinned spirits (who went with great reluctance, still unconvinced they should give up their freshly acquired flesh), and rushed for the abandoned station, where the glimmering carriages were just pulling in.

This time, they did not stop to get tickets.

Alice and Benyamin shoved the lot of them into as many carriages as necessary before hauling Laylee, her barrow, and Oliver into another carriage. Once certain that Laylee was in control and still in communication with her drifting spirits, Alice and Benyamin hopped inside, squeezing themselves into the tight space, determined to stick together this time, no matter the discomfort.

Alice, as usual, wasted no time.

Laylee was feeling better than ever, but Alice was determined to heal her until she was completely cured, and with an hour and a half to go until they reached the castle, there was still a great deal to be done. Benyamin and Oliver lifted Laylee out of the barrow to lay her down on the bench seat, and Alice set to work. In no time at all, she was, again, making visible progress. Alice had already returned Laylee's arms and legs back to normal, but now she was working on Laylee's face. In the last several hours, her skin had gone from a warm, golden brown to an ashy, dusty shade of rust, and as Alice pressed her fingers to the mordeshoor's skin, one gentle movement at a time, Laylee slowly came back to life. Her eyes were closed, but Alice could see the rapid movement behind her eyelids, and only after she was satisfied with the color coming back into Laylee's cheeks did Alice finally remove her hands for a quick rest. It was tiring work, after all, and Alice was out of breath with exhaustion—and exhilaration. It was gratifying to see her hard work pay off, and it was even more gratifying when Laylee flickered open her eyes, and her friends finally saw her real eye color.

Gone was the cold silver gaze of the mordeshoor Alice and Oliver had only known, and in its stead were the warm amber eyes of a girl who, for the first time in over a year, was able to see clearly. Laylee, who could not understand exactly what had happened, but could *feel* the difference, sat straight up and wept. It was an extraordinary change, and a gift she'd not been prepared to receive. She looked at her hands, no longer trembling, and her legs, no longer aching, and she threw herself into Alice's arms and cried.

By the time they reached the castle, Laylee was standing up. She was grateful for her health, but she couldn't help but feel a deep pain in her gut for the four lives they'd lost this evening. Alice was sure that Laylee would, in the end, be ready to smile again, but Laylee couldn't bring herself to be happy yet. There was still too much work to do—and she could only guess at the repercussions she would face for their losses tonight.

So it was with an unsettling grimness that she prepared to wash the last of her remaining dead, and it was with a heaviness in her step that she jumped off the glass carriage and into the train station and ran, strong and skillful, toward home.

(With many strange bodies following closely behind.)

✦

It seemed clear what needed to be done.

Laylee charged directly into the backyard, her small army following, and prepared the tub. The spirits who'd stolen human skins needed a bit more persuasion to give up their new clothes, but after several minutes of show-and-tell on the part of the mordeshoor, they were eventually convinced they'd made a terrible mistake. Good thing, too, as they would have to go first. Laylee quickly separated their fourteen corpses from the large pile in her shed, and got to work.

Friends, it was a very, very long night.

They scrubbed until their fingers bled and their eyelids frosted open. They scrubbed until they couldn't speak and could barely stand. They scrubbed until Benyamin's mother showed up, hobbling forward disappointed and exhausted, with no volunteers in tow (none could be persuaded to help, I'm afraid), and still Laylee would not sit. She stood tall, scrubbing bodies until her fingernails broke, and as each body was shipped off to the Otherwhere, the corresponding spirit, duly shamed, stepped out of the human skin they awkwardly wore, and left it lying in the snow. Only then did Benyamin's insects disembark their human ship, and allow the body to reclaim its flesh. They did this until all fourteen humans were reunited with their skins, and even then, Laylee would not stop.

Alice feared the mordeshoor had been reinvigorated just in time to destroy herself all over again. And though her friends begged her to stop, to slow down, to take a break before she grew ill, Laylee would not hesitate, she would not listen to reason, and she thought that she would rather die than live with the weight of this burden or this grief ever again. So she soldiered ahead, working with her friends—and even occasionally alone—until every single body was scrubbed and sent off into the night.

✦

Only then, dear friends, did Laylee Layla Fenjoon finally fall.

FORGIVE ME,
BUT THINGS
ONLY GET
WORSE

Polygons of light broke through damp branches, tree trunks perspiring in the misty dawn. It was a cold, golden morning, the sun unfurling its rays to touch pinpricks of dew, the rolling hills rumbling under blankets of snow. For a protracted moment, everything was new, untouched; the horrors of the prior evening were temporarily forgotten. It was that impossible time between sleep and consciousness, when fears were still too tired to exist, when responsibilities stood patiently behind a door. Laylee was loath to disturb this peace, but she could feel herself stir; she was becoming increasingly aware of sounds and surroundings, and she was now dimly aware of the fact that she'd fallen asleep in the snow. It was odd, then, that she felt warm and heavy—like someone had thought to throw a cloak over her as she slept— and it was only when, finally, reluctantly, she blinked open her eyes that she realized she was not covered in blankets, but in bugs—tens of hundreds of hard-bodied creatures—who had curled up quietly against her skin. Somehow, even in the face of this revolting realization, Laylee couldn't help but smile. In fact, Alice swears she heard Laylee laugh out loud (she claims it's the sound that woke her that morning), but Laylee has repeatedly denied this.

Our point here is that Laylee, though conflicted about the mixed outcome of the prior evening's events, felt the crippling burden of her corpses slough off her body as if she'd shed a full skin. She felt a lightness she hadn't experienced in years, and as she became aware not only of the day, but of the healthy strength in her limbs, she allowed herself to feel—if only for a moment—*happy*. The evening had been a horrible one, but at least it was over. They'd saved as many innocent people as they could from an exceptionally dire fate, and sent off all the outstanding spirits to the Otherwhere. But it was with a sinking feeling that she sat up slowly, delicately dislodging insects from her eyebrows. Laylee still felt a kick to her gut when she thought of the four lives they hadn't saved, and though she'd never be able to applaud her own actions, she did manage to feel proud of her friends for working so hard to help her last night. So when Alice mumbled a smiling *good morning* in her direction, Laylee felt her face stretch in an entirely new way, cheeks and chin fighting to accommodate a rare grin that brightened her amber eyes. Laylee looked up at the sky, waved her own hello to the winter birds who'd gathered, as usual, for their morning conference, and allowed herself to imagine what on earth she'd do with a day off.

It was just then that Laylee heard someone call her name.

She stumbled up to her feet, wild-eyed, at the sound of Baba's voice, and spun around in search of him. She felt her heart leap up into her throat until she was sure she would choke on it, fear and happiness erupting within her. Baba had come home.

Baba had come *home.*

At first, all she saw was his face. All she heard was the thrumming in her head; all she felt was the impossible stillness of the air around her. Her mind had gone thick and muddy, so strange and dense she could rake her fingers through it as she clawed her way toward him. She wanted answers, she wanted to be angry, she wanted to hit him, she wanted a hug.

Baba was *here.* And at first, that was all she saw.

She did not question why his hands were hidden behind his back. She did not see the Town Elders congregated behind him. She couldn't feel Oliver tugging at her arm. She didn't hear Alice suddenly scream. She wouldn't notice Benyamin and his mother duck out of sight without a word, too decent to stick their noses in Laylee's business.

Baba was standing in front of her, and at first this was all that mattered.

❖

What happens next is difficult to relay.

Laylee still can't speak of this time in any measure of detail, so I will endeavor to piece together as comprehensive a summary as I'm able:

The Whichwood Elders had descended upon Laylee's home at first light, determined to finally put an end to the mordeshoor business. They did not see Laylee's work as even the smallest kind of success, you see. They saw the events of the evening prior as a terrible wake-up call—a horrifying reminder of the dangers of relying upon mordeshoors. The Elders had long felt that this, the work of the mordeshoor, was an outmoded system for dealing with the dead—it was an ancient ritual they'd held on to for simple reasons of maintaining tradition. Most other magical lands had long ago dispensed with traditional methods of dispatching the dead; they'd enacted new measures, overruled the old magic with more modern magical systems. Mordeshoors were near extinction, after all, and Laylee Layla Fenjoon—who, after Baba, would be the last of her line—was already widely considered to be terrible at her job.

The Town Elders had decided that someone had to be held accountable for last night's devastation. What Laylee saw as a difficult save of a terrible evening, the town saw only as ruination. Four innocent people had died. Many more had been stripped of their flesh in front of their own children while insects rampaged said flesh without permission; ghosts had scandalized the city into mass chaos, and scores of people had been so traumatized by the ordeal that they'd been rushed to the hospital. The people were outraged and terrified—a lethal combination for an angry mob—and in their blind rage, they were demanding justice. Someone was to pay for the sins of the evening, and Laylee, at only thirteen years old, was deemed too young.

Baba had been sentenced to death.

He'd let this happen, they'd decided. He'd abandoned his post to a child, and the entire system had fallen apart. It was his fault that the people of Whichwood had been compromised and four of them had been killed mercilessly in the street. It was Baba's fault that Laylee had been so overworked. It was Baba's fault for putting the town in danger—for being so irresponsible—and he would be punished for it.

The Elders had found the alleged criminal sitting in a tree, eating a sheaf of paper. They'd bound him and brought him before his daughter because he was allowed one concession before his impending death: to be able to say good-bye to his loved ones. And so here he was, so thin and scraggly Laylee hardly recognized him, and he stared at her, a little happy and a little confused, and smiled.

Laylee closed her eyes.

She would not stir; she would not breathe or bat an eyelash; she would not speak; she would not cry or gasp or ever, ever be moved from this spot. She froze because she hoped that the world would freeze, too, that time would fall over and crush her, that if she simply waited long enough, this pain could all be undone.

"Laylee *joonam*," Baba said. "*Azizeh delam*."

Tears welled up in her heart, her throat, her pockets.

"*Azizam*," Baba said again. "*Azizam*, please look at me."

Finally, she felt her mouth move. The seam of her lips had gone dry; her jaw throbbed in her skull. "*I will not*," she whispered.

She heard the sound of metal—a key? A few clicks. The distinct sounds of manacles clanging open and closed.

And then—

A warm hand against her face.

Laylee opened her eyes, tears streaming down her cheeks. She wore no expression as her heart exploded in her chest, as her father stood before her and said, "Laylee, I finally found him."

"No," she tried to say. "*No*," but it wouldn't come out.

"He finally came to me this morning," Baba said, all gums and glittering eyes, "and told me we'd speak soon."

Laylee felt her limbs grow thick and heavy, her veins knotting under her skin.

"I told you," said Baba, smiling, "I told you I'd find him, *azizam*."

He was talking about Death, of course. Baba had left two years ago to find Death and had never returned. It was his great mission—to find the creature responsible for taking his wife. And now Death had promised him an audience, and Baba couldn't understand why.

Everything happened very quickly after that.

The Elders dragged Baba away, telling Laylee that she could visit him in his cell just before his public humiliation later that evening. He would stand in chains before a crowd as a very dark magic reached into his chest and disintegrated the heart beating within him. It was a simple procedure, they'd said. *Shouldn't be* too *painful,* they'd said. They assured her he would be dead before sunset.

Laylee nodded without meaning to—wondering all the while what had compelled her to do so—and looked at no one and nothing as her life was dismantled before her. The decision to sentence Baba to death had not only been made quickly and without ceremony, it had been pushed through as an emergency ruling in favor of an angry mob demanding justice. This, the execution of her father, was done as a supposed kindness to Laylee, because after Baba was dead, Laylee's punishment would be far less severe: she would be put on trial for treason.

"Once the anger of the people has been sated with the blood of your father, they might be willing to listen to your cause," she remembered someone saying to her.

She was told she'd be given an opportunity to defend herself, her actions, and the necessity of her profession in court, but that this was not a guarantee of anything. If the jury ruled in favor of the people, Laylee's entire purpose as a magical person would shatter, and there was nothing she could do about it. It was a clause—a protection in the old magic—that, in the case of danger or disaster, the results of a proper court trial could overturn ancient magical tradition. It was a judicial process that had never before seemed threatening.

But now?

Laylee had gone numb in parts of her face.

Alice and Oliver were by her side, holding her upright, and though both Alice and Oliver say they tried to hug her, to speak to her—to offer words of comfort—Laylee claims she heard nothing.

You might now be wondering why none of the children had tried to stop the Elders from taking Baba—after all, together they could do quite a bit of powerful magic—and you'd be well within your right to wonder. But the situation with Baba was much more complicated in the moment than it might have seemed. It all happened so quickly—and it was such a shocking revelation—that it had rendered the group of them temporarily impotent. Suddenly, in the face of a towering group of power-ful and angry Elders, Alice and Oliver and Laylee felt fully their age—too young and too old all at once. Laylee felt small. She remembers feeling scared.

She remembers sitting somewhere inside of her house.

She remembers walking in, somehow, and she remembers Maman screeching at her. "Where have you been? I was wor-ried sick! Who was that out there? Who are these children you've brought into our home? Laylee—*Laylee*—"

She remembers the birds tapping at her windows, their sharp beaks pecking ceaselessly, and she remembers someone reaching into her chest and ripping out her heart, and she re-members exhaustion, she remembers blurriness. And there was something else; she remembers something else, too—

"Oh, no!" Alice gasped, reaching for Oliver's arm.

"What is it?" he hissed, wrenching his arm away from her. "You're cutting off my circulation, Alice, good grief—"

"Father is here."

Oliver Newbanks jumped two feet in the air. His first thought was to hide, but there was no time. It seemed a perfect coincidence that Alice had looked out the window at precisely the right moment to see her father strolling up to the door of Laylee's castle, but the fact that Father was here was far from fortuitous. Father's arrival in Whichwood could only mean that Alice and Oliver had ruined everything. The thing was,

Ferenwood parents never came to collect their children in the middle of a task—not even in the face of failure. It was up to the children to deal with the tasks on their own. That Father had come to fetch Alice meant that she was in very, very deep trouble. (And Oliver, who'd run away from home to accompany her, was about to be caught and thoroughly punished.)

Laylee doesn't remember much more than this.

She doesn't remember meeting Alice's father; she doesn't remember his condolences or his assurances that he'd tried desperately to convince the Whichwood Elders to change their minds. She doesn't remember his offer to take her away with them to Ferenwood.

She remembers staring at a wall.

She remembers, vaguely, the terrified look on Oliver's face. She remembers him taking her hand; she remembers staring at his fingers as he said good-bye.

She doesn't remember Alice and Oliver leaving.

Laylee cannot remember what anything else looked like that afternoon. She says she sat down and did not move or even cry. She says the hours she spent waiting for Baba to die were the longest hours she's ever lived. And though she went to see her father later that evening, she cannot remember how her feet got her there.

Baba was not unhappy when he died.

Laylee watched him as he waved at her, a deep resignation rounding his shoulders. He was lost in conversation just before it happened, speaking animatedly with a spirit no one but she and he could see. Death stood beside him, gentle and tall, and held Baba close as Baba's eyes went wide and—with a sudden, choking gasp—he lost the ability to speak. Only then did Death finally, patiently, answer all of Baba's questions.

Not long before it ended, Baba smiled.

Laylee watched on silently, stone-faced, as her father's knees buckled, his body folding into itself like a series of closing doors. She would not speak, not even as her skin seemed to turn inside out in agony. She didn't shed a single tear as the people booed and threw old food at the broken body of a man who'd raised her on a diet of honey and poetry. She would not betray a single emotion as the mob shouted obscenities at her, as they rushed around her, yanking at her cloak, making fun of her bones, spitting on her boots and bloody clothes.

She wouldn't miss a moment of her father's last day.

This, she would remember.

✤

Just before, Baba had held her hand through the bars of his cell and cried. He said, "Laylee it's happening—he's near—can you feel him?"

"Yes, Baba," she'd whispered, squeezing his fingers. "He's just outside."

"You saw him?" Baba said anxiously. "What did you think?"

"He seems kind and very sad," said Laylee. "But I think he likes you."

Baba beamed and sat back on his bench, eyes filled with wonder.

No one spoke for a while after that. Baba was lost in his thoughts, and Laylee was just—lost. Untethered.

Finally, Baba said, "He said he would take me to your mother."

Laylee looked up.

Baba's eyes had filled with tears. "It would be so good to see her," he said, choking on the words. "Heaven knows, I miss her so much. I miss her every day."

And Laylee fought back a wave of pain so unbearable it nearly took her breath away.

Had he not missed *her*?

Laylee had been at home, quietly surviving and hardly alive all these years he'd been gone, and her father had never returned. She did not seem to be enough—she knew now that Baba would never love her as much as he loved her mother—and she felt the pain of this realization torch a path down her throat, unshed tears singeing the whites of her eyes.

Oh, reader, if only you knew how dearly Laylee loved him—if only you could understand how she adored this flawed, broken man who knew not how to father. She'd loved him in spite of himself; she'd loved him for reasons impractical and unreasonable. She'd *loved,* you see, and loving was an action nearly impossible to undo, and so, with her broken heart she grieved: first, for herself, for the child whose parent loved his spouse more than his kin, and second, for Baba, for the man who'd lost his way, his self, and the love of his life too soon.

The guards came, then. Baba's time was up.

Laylee grabbed for him one last time, a desperate attempt to hold him here, in this world, where even she knew he no longer belonged. Baba was so calm. He took her little hand in his and smiled his big, gummy smile. He then reached into his pocket and poured, into her outstretched hand, the remainder of his teeth.

Laylee looked at him.

"If you plant them, they will grow," was all he said, and closed her fist around the gift.

In the end, the guards were forced to drag her away.

She does not remember screaming.

✦

Now Death had fallen to his knees and wrapped his arms around her father's withered limbs the way a parent might comfort a child—it was a tender, careful gesture, an embrace that begged the body to be unafraid. And when Laylee saw the final breath leave her father's lungs, she froze.

Laylee Layla Fenjoon was still a mordeshoor, after all. She watched, with bated breath, as Baba's spirit separated from his skin. She knew that soon—very soon—he would follow her back to the castle, so she turned suddenly on her heel, her red cloak whipping around her in a perfect circle, and walked tall, shoulders back, head held high even as screams built homes inside her, and headed in the direction of home.

The Elders had promised to send Baba's body back to her, which meant that tonight she would prepare a coffin for her father.

Maman had not bothered to say good-bye.

In fact, Maman had not said anything at all to her after Baba arrived in the castle. She and Baba were so overjoyed to have found each other again that Laylee, who had come to accept the unpalatable truth that her parents had loved each other far more than they'd ever loved her, could no longer find the energy to be upset. Maman and Baba were finally at peace, and Laylee could see now that it was not that they did not *like* her—it was just that their own happiness was so large it had left little room in their hearts for others. So when Laylee awoke the next morning to perfect silence, she knew, instinctively, that Maman had followed Baba into the Otherwhere. The wailing spirit was gone—which meant the book of her mother's life had finally, peacefully closed—and Laylee, who was too close to death to ever purposely misunderstand it, was running out of excuses to be angry.

For years Maman's rampages had given Laylee daily ammunition to be irritated, Baba's carelessness had given her ample reason to feel furious and entitled, and her work—her life's work—had afforded her every opportunity to stew in bitterness and resentment.

But now?

There were no ghosts, no corpses, no parents or strange friends, no illnesses to worry about. Laylee looked ahead and saw a black, gaping nothingness stretch out before her, and the immensity of it—the overwhelming grasp of it—threatened to devour her.

It was then that Laylee fell to her knees and felt her chest split open.

Sobs ripped through her body with a raw, ferocious pain unlike any she'd ever allowed herself to experience. She sobbed until she couldn't breathe, until her eyes had swollen shut, until her throat had gone raw from gasping, until her body had run out of tears. She had finally allowed herself to feel the pain she'd hidden from herself all these years, and she grieved, she grieved for the life she'd had, for the life she'd lost, for the years she'd wasted being inward and angry, for the friends she could've had, for the job she should've cherished—

Oh, she missed it all desperately.

In the end, it was the weight of a single truth that finally broke her:

Reader, she had been ungrateful.

COME,
LET'S LEAVE
THIS PLACE
FOR A BIT

Oliver Newbanks could not be consoled. Alice had tried and failed, repeatedly, to console him, and her failure to do so should come as a surprise to no one, given the fact that Alice had been crying hysterically as she attempted to reassure the boy, through hiccuping sobs, not to worry. Father, too, could not be moved to console Oliver Newbanks, as he was still busy being terribly disappointed in the both of them.

So it is here that we come to pivot again in our story:

Here, on an underwater elevator moving at such a clip as to be concerning; here, as Oliver Newbanks sits quietly with his head bowed and his hands clasped between his legs. This underwater elevator is new, an intentionally kept secret recently uncovered; instead of the usual five-day sojourn, their trip home will take only two. Alice and Oliver find even this truncated length of time abhorrent, and the modern comforts of the shiny transport go unappreciated by those who occupy its interior. They've been traveling for just under twenty-four hours now and Alice's attentions are still focused on her incessant weeping; Oliver, on the other hand, has squeezed his eyes shut, his vision clouded by anger and heartbreak; Father, whose age has armored him against the dangers of needless overexcitement, can only bring himself to occasionally interrupt his daughter's histrionics long enough to sigh and pat her knee.

Here, we pivot, because we will leave the mordeshoor and her world for a short time.

I will not engage you in the many private details of her pain, as I feel she's earned the right to a respite from our prying. But I find it important to note that we pick up with our Ferenwood friends at the same hour we leave Laylee behind. In fact, at precisely the moment Laylee falls to her knees and feels her chest split open, Oliver Newbanks is assaulted by a pain so sudden he jolts forward in his seat. And it is here, as he sits unsteadily, chest heaving, not comprehending *why* it is he feels his heart tearing at the seams, that we are reunited with him in his mind.

❖

Oliver Newbanks could not understand what was happening to him.

He'd come along on this journey for a bit of good fun and little more—but nothing had gone according to plan. Indeed, it had been—from start to finish—an unequivocally miserable experience compounded by Oliver's newly minted fear: that he'd managed to damage his heart in some irreparable way. The damage in question came at regular, painful, intervals, with no signs of abating. The very first pangs had arrived the moment he'd set eyes on Laylee—though back then he'd thought it a fluke. Soon he began to feel ill around her all the time, nervous and off balance; from there, the symptoms had grown only more severe. Now, even with a vast body of water between them, he felt worse than ever. Short of breath. Sick to his stomach.

Just weeks ago he hadn't even known she existed.

The first time Alice told him about the girl she was meant to help, Alice had mispronounced Laylee's name. Catching herself, Alice had repeated the moniker several times to get it right. Oliver found himself unconsciously mimicking the action, rolling Laylee's name around in his mouth, enjoying the sound, the shape of it.

He had not expected her to strike pain into his heart.

And now, halfway home and ostensibly losing his mind, all Oliver could think about was getting back to Whichwood. He was anxious to arrive home if only to find a way to return to Laylee on his own this time—alone—without the weeping Alice, who, I feel I should note, had begun weeping shortly after Father had explained, not unkindly, how thoroughly she'd failed her task.

Oliver did not think he could stomach another twenty-four hours of her tears.

It was not that he was heartless; Oliver knew how devastating it was to fail a task. He could imagine the humiliation Alice would face upon arriving home. Alice had been dragged back by the Town Elders for having caused such a riotous disaster as to require a chaperoned return into town by her own father. It was beyond mortifying—it was unheard of. He felt deeply sorry for her. And Oliver would never say this aloud, of course, but he quietly wondered whether such a level of ridicule was even survivable.

But there was another part of him, a part of him that he would never acknowledge—would never credit with truth— that wondered (rather callously) whether Alice didn't deserve such shaming. After all, it was true that Alice could have done better. That she should have *been* better.

Alice had done just about everything wrong.

"When you win a Surrender," Father had explained to them earlier, "you're awarded a five—the highest possible score— which means you're considered the most capable of your year. Earning a five, as you did," he said now only to Alice, "meant that your task would be far more complicated than the tasks of your peers."

"I know," said Alice in a hurry. "And it was, Father, it—"

Father shook his head. "*Much* more complicated, Alice. Washing dead bodies, restoring a supply of deteriorated magic"— he waved a hand—"these tasks are difficult, yes, but fairly uncomplicated. There's no nuance in these actions, only repetition. You were expected to think more complexly, my dear."

Alice blinked at him.

"You solved the obvious issue," he said gently. "You chose the easy fix."

"But, Father," said Alice, "it wasn't easy—we didn't even know she was sick for some time—"

Again, Father shook his head.

"It was a test, darling." He smiled, sadness pinching his eyes. "Would you choose the problem your hands could easily solve? Or would you recognize the illusion set before you for what it was: a distraction, nothing more."

"But she was dying," Alice said breathlessly, desperately. "I had to keep her from dying, didn't I? Otherwise I wouldn't have been able to help at all!"

"My sweet girl—don't you see?" Father took her hand. "There were always *two* parts to her healing process."

Alice was silent for a long time. Finally, she whispered, "No, Father. I don't understand."

It was only then that Oliver, who could not take it anymore, interjected (with a measure of anger) and said, "Laylee needed color, yes, but she also needed a *friend,* Alice. She needed real *help.* Not a bandage."

Alice turned to him, eyes now brimming with tears, and said, "I thought—I th-thought I was helping her—"

Father spoke sympathetically when he said, "What you did for Laylee took only a matter of hours; in that short time, you created a temporary solution to a much larger problem. And by ignoring the larger issue, you unwittingly set into motion the collapse of Laylee's entire life." Father sighed as he spoke, closing his eyes in a show of deep exhaustion. "When we send our children on a task," he explained, "we expect them to do work that will take much longer than a few hours, Alice—we expect them to be gone for many months. We hope for their work to be truly restorative; we hope they'll bestow an ever-lasting kindness upon the person or place they've helped. Laylee would have healed—at a much slower, but more permanent rate—had you only helped ease her burden a little more every day. With you there by her side, she might have learned to slow down, to take breaks—to stand up to the townspeople who'd taken advantage of her—and, eventually, slow the effects of the illness spreading through her body." Father hesitated. Studied his daughter. "Don't you see, my Alice? The Town Elders recognized in you *two* great talents: one was your gift with colors, yes, but the other was your heart."

"My heart?" said Alice.

Father smiled. "Yes, my dear. Your heart. The Elders found your burgeoning, complicated friendship with Oliver—who, forgive me," Father said, glancing at Oliver, "was once a decidedly difficult character—"

Oliver frowned.

"—to be of deep interest. You both built that relationship against the turbulent background of the twisted, complicated world of Furthermore, a world known mostly for tearing people apart. That you managed to forge something beautiful from the madness was deeply admirable. And ultimately," Father said, "we all hoped you'd be able to do the same for Laylee. Your task was always to heal her in two ways: with your hands *and* with your heart. You would have earned her trust and become a friend upon whom she would one day rely, healing her from the inside out. In the end it is your gift of time—and of compassion—that's most invaluable to a person in pain, my darling. It's true that you left her with a healthy body," he said finally, "but Laylee's spirit is now more tortured than ever."

And Alice, ashamed of herself and afraid for her future, had not ceased her weeping, not even to speak.

❖

Alice and Oliver spent the rest of the trip home in silence. Oliver tried to drown out her keening with the roar of his own regrets—and managed nicely for a while—but it was just as he braced himself against another shuddering wave of pain that he wondered, with increasing agitation, whether he'd ever forgive himself for what they'd done.

He had to find a way to make things right.

Oliver Newbanks knew himself to be just as culpable as Alice. He knew he'd played a critical role in what transpired with Laylee, and he couldn't shake these fears loose from his brain. It was, after all, because of them that Laylee's spirits had gone free. If he and Alice had never shown up, Laylee would never have abandoned her ghosts—she'd never have attended Yalda. Even so, their presence could have been more of a help to her. If only they'd stayed at the castle—if only they hadn't been so selfish and impatient—if only they'd *listened* to Laylee when she'd finally mustered the courage to ask for their help—

Oh, Oliver would never forgive himself.

He could have prevented all of this from happening. The group of them could have worked tirelessly through those first few nights to dispatch Laylee's dead. They could've put to bed the possibility of angry souls ever seeking revenge. They could've been more understanding of the difficulties of Laylee's life.

If only, he said to himself, over and over again. *If only.*

It was their fault that her father had been killed. It was because of them that Laylee was about to lose everything. He and Alice had forced their way into Laylee's life and ruined all that had ever mattered to her. Never mind the fact that he would never forgive himself—

What if *Laylee* never forgave him?

It was still spring in Ferenwood. Springtime was always the season for the annual Surrender and, as Alice and Oliver had not been gone very long (careful readers will note that time passes in identical increments in Ferenwood and Whichwood, despite their different seasons), the two friends returned home to find their fresh, blooming spring weather still intact. It was a bit of a shock, really, this abrupt transition between winter and spring, and it took a bit of getting used to.

As the three of them disembarked the elevator at the edge of town, they were met by an audience of angry Town Elders whose dour facial expressions said everything Alice and Oliver needed to know. The Elders spoke loudly and angrily, gesticulating for effect as they made grave pronouncements of disappointment, and finished it all by handing both Alice and Oliver a sealed envelope containing the details of the official hearing they'd be required to attend. Apparently the two friends had broken several cross-magical ordinances and would have to be seen by a judge who would decide upon a suitable punishment. Nothing too serious, of course—as they were underage—but perhaps several weeks of community service or some such. Alice cried and clung to her father, visibly remorseful. Oliver couldn't be bothered to care.

He was instructed by the Elders to head home straightaway, where they were sure his parents would dole out their own punishments. Oliver nearly laughed out loud. He had the magic of *persuasion*—he hadn't been punished since he'd learned how to speak.

Alice's mother was standing quietly by, and as Father and Alice broke free to meet her, Oliver found himself suddenly alone. No one would be coming for him. He'd long ago destroyed any hopes of having a healthy relationship with his family by too often distorting their minds with persuasion. He'd discovered his magic at too young and too immature an age, and he'd used it against his parents as frequently as he saw fit—regularly entrancing them for weeks at a time so that Oliver had been able to come and go and do as he pleased. Just last year Alice had helped him recognize the error of his ways, and Oliver finally came clean to his family, hoping to repair the damage. Sadly, his parents had been frightened by him, and theirs had been a painful conversation. Oliver knew now that it would be a long time before he would regain their trust.

Now his parents kept a polite distance from their only child;

they were still getting to know him—still relearning their re-lationship. In many ways Oliver, at fourteen years old, was a veritable stranger to them. And this was the source of a deep and terrible regret that kept our brooding friend from using his magic as much as he used to.

Oliver sighed, shoved one hand into his pocket, and grimaced as he waved good-bye to a tearful Alice. He'd be in touch with her soon enough, he was sure, but he couldn't help but wonder how she'd be punished for her failures. For now, it was best they went their separate ways.

And so they did.

Oliver ducked his head as he walked, shoulders tense and rounded, and failed to notice the beautiful land he lived in. The tall grass danced against his legs as he moved and he shud-dered at the touch, jerking away; butterflies fluttered against his fingers and he flicked them off, grumbling; the sun was high and jolly and warm and Oliver, irritated, muttered an ungentlemanly word under his breath. He'd never missed the cold so much.

Spring weather did not suit his state of mind.

Oliver was soon annoyed by everything—the soothing sounds of nearby rivers, the cheerful flowers that flanked him, the bright leaves of faraway trees swaying carelessly in the wind. He found himself snapping at a large bird that had landed on his shoulder, shouting at the poor creature so suddenly that it took flight in a hurry, its talons catching and tearing at his shirt. It was unlike him to be so uncharitable to the world. It was unlike him to be seen without a smile.

But Whichwood had bewitched him, and now that Oliver was home again he wanted, once more, to run away.

Ferenwood had never felt quite right to him. It had always been a size too small for his spirit—not so uncomfortable that he could not bear it, but just uncomfortable enough to be constantly on his mind. Oliver strained against the safe idyll of Ferenwood. It was a lovely town, yes—predictably so—but Oliver tired of the pleasant people and their unbounded kindness. He'd been hounded for years by an incessant whisper that begged him to explore extraordinary places, to look for complexity in people and spaces—and it was for precisely this reason that he'd enjoyed Furthermore so much.* Oliver wanted to get lost on purpose. He wanted to have baffling conversations with strangers; he wanted to learn new languages and eat food he'd never heard of and—well, the simple truth was that he didn't feel about Ferenwood the way that Alice did. Alice loved it there with every bit of her soul. She was a Ferenwood girl from foot to forehead, and she would be happy there, in that colorful land, for the rest of her life.

---

* You will remember my mentioning earlier that Furthermore is the name of another neighboring magical land explored in a previous novel, one that introduces us to Alice and Oliver and the rather tumultuous start to their friendship.

But Oliver wanted more.

He missed Whichwood—and one young lady in particular—with a painful kind of longing, and Oliver Newbanks, who had not the faintest idea how to get back to it or her (the underwater elevator being accessible only by Town Elders), had never, not in his whole life, ever been in such a foul temper.**

** I've recounted this part of the story to Laylee several times now, and she never tires of hearing it. If I didn't know any better, I'd swear she was secretly proud of having inspired such sulkiness in Oliver's otherwise upbeat character. She denies this, of course.

Home **was such a funny word.**

Oliver's had never felt like much, but there it was, waiting for him in the distance. He trudged on with a sigh. Not moments after entering the quiet abode and waving hello to the parents who sat calmly in the kitchen, sipping raspberry teas and reading the local newspaper—

The headline read **LOCAL COW TRAPPED IN OWN MANURE**

—Oliver locked himself in his bedroom, flung himself onto his bed, and pressed the heels of his shaking hands against his eyes.

He felt angry and ill; he felt strange all over. He felt—he felt—what was it? This sensation?

He had never been so upset, so frustrated, so powerless in all his life. He hated the limitations of his young body, of his dependence upon his parents and the system designed to hold him. He felt like he might explode out of his own skin, like he contained galaxies no one would ever see, like he'd been made privy to one of life's greatest secrets and he would keep that secret, carry it inside of him forever. What *was* this, this tenderness in his bones? This earthquake breaking open his chest to make room for his newer, larger heart? Oliver did not know that what he felt now was the beginning of something greater than himself. All he knew, with sudden, piercing clarity, was that he would never be the same.

What was *happening* to him?

Oliver had no way of knowing this then—if he had, I wonder whether he would consider a revision—but the poor boy would ask himself this exact question no fewer than a thousand times over the course of the next four years. This is how long it would take him to get Laylee Layla Fenjoon to take a single, serious step in his direction. It would be four years before she looked at him like he wanted her to, four years before she smiled and said, without speaking, that she loved him.

He would wait four years for a moment that lasted no longer than five seconds; a moment that would change the course of his entire life.

But for now, he was only fourteen years old.

And right now, there was a bird knocking at his window.

It was the same large bird that had tried to sit on his shoulder—the one who'd ripped Oliver's shirt on his walk home. He recognized its iridescent purple feathers and long white beak, but just because he recognized the bird did not mean he wasn't wary of it. He had no idea why a bird would be knocking at his window—as far as Oliver was aware, this wasn't a common practice of Ferenwoodian birds—but his curiosity got the better of him.

Reluctantly, he inched his way toward the single large window in his bedroom, and pressed his hands against the glass.

"What do you want?" he said.

The bird would only knock.

"What is it?" he shout-whispered.

Again, the bird pecked at the glass.

Frustrated, Oliver shoved open his window, ready to shoo it away by hand, when he was accosted, all at once, by a swarm of spiders. What happens next will go down in history as one of the single most terrifying experiences of Oliver's life—and this he does not deny. In the time it took Oliver to prepare to scream ("I wasn't going to scream," he said to me), a hundred spiders had already spun a series of webs around his head, gagging his mouth shut. Oliver thought he might die of fright. He tried to call for help, all to no avail. He flung his arms around to try and knock the spiders off, but there were too many to fight. And now that he'd been safely rendered speechless, the rest of the arachnids felt free to work on binding his arms and legs. Only once his limbs had been thoroughly secured did the spiders then lift Oliver's body onto their backs and shuttle him out the window, where the violet-feathered bird snatched him up in her talons and set off to sea.

To be clear: It was simply not true that Alice Alexis Queensmeadow had spent the forty-eight hours of their trip home weeping hysterically. Oliver, Alice assured me, had grossly exaggerated the facts. She had wept, it was true—but she had not lost control of her faculties. The very opposite, in fact.

Alice had been *thinking.*

Surely, those readers who remember Alice's adventures in Furthermore would agree that she is not a girl easily cowed into submission. Certainly not. Alice had a heart of silk and a spine of steel; her tears did not render her incapable of kicking a person in the teeth if need be. And now, more upset and more determined than ever, she knew she had to find a way to set things right for Laylee. She had to get back to Whichwood—but how?

It was still only morning, but her parents had sent her directly to her room and forbade her from coming out except for mealtimes and visits to the toilet. She was to sit here, in the small room she shared with her three younger brothers (who were currently at school), and think about what she'd done.

Well, she'd already done that. And Alice was growing impatient.

Alice's home, much like Benyamin's, was decidedly small—so small, in fact, that she worried any unexpected sound might travel through to the adjoining room and alert her parents of her intentions to be obstinate—and so these last several minutes she'd been engaged in a herculean effort to sit uncommonly still. She counted seconds under her breath, sitting on her hands as she mouthed the numbers, holding steady just long enough to lull her mother and father into a false sense of security. Only after a suitable period of silence had passed did she then, carefully—very carefully—tiptoe to her bedroom door and place her ear against the wood, listening for her parents' voices. Once she was sure they were far enough away, she reached into her pocket and extracted the wriggling stowaway hidden therein.

Haftpa, the seven-legged spider, perched proudly in the palm of her hand.

"Hello, friend," she whispered, and smiled.

Haftpa waved a leg.

"Is he here yet?" she said softly.

Haftpa jumped up and down in her hand.

"Is that a yes?" said Alice. "Do you know where he is?"

Again, Haftpa jumped up and down.

"Alright then," Alice said. "I'll pack my bags, do a quick bit of magic, and we'll be off. You'll stay close, won't you?"

The peacock spider bounced around once more, only too happy to acquiesce. He'd come to adore this pale girl in the short time he'd known her, and he'd never been so excited to play an integral role in an adventure. And so it was with a happy hurry that he scurried across Alice's arm, around her elbow, past her shoulder and up the side of her neck, and settled comfortably behind her left ear.

Now—it should be known that Alice did not *want* to use her magic against her parents. She was generally a very compliant child who loved her family (and her father, in particular) with an emotional overabundance uncommon in thirteen-year-olds. But Alice felt that the situation had left her with no choice. She needed to leave Ferenwood immediately, and Father would never have allowed it. Later, she said to herself, she'd happily accept a hefty punishment for her crimes—but for now she'd had to make an executive decision, and a simple twitch of her mind was enough to do the trick.

Suddenly, everything went black.

Alice's ability to manipulate and manifest color was impressive in a myriad of ways, but her talent was perhaps most extraordinary when she used it to diminish the pigment in the world around her. Just now she'd snuffed out all the colors in her home—and in her parents' bodies—plunging their small world into complete blackness. Her parents would know what she'd done, of course, but it was just enough of a distraction for her to grab her rucksack, run out the door, and hear the frantic voices of her mother and father shouting for her to *get back here this instant, young lady!*

By the time she reversed the magic, Alice would be long gone.

I feel I should explain.

The morning she'd been forced to leave Whichwood, Alice Alexis Queensmeadow (and her trusty companion, Benyamin Felankasak) had already set into motion the clinging beginnings of a contingency plan. Benyamin's mother had tried (*tried* being the operative word here) to drag her son away from that morning's emotional scene as soon as she saw what was happening—Madarjoon thought Laylee should be allowed her privacy—but Benyamin, who'd been horrified and heartbroken by all he'd heard, could not make himself leave. Ultimately, he compromised by staying just far enough away—pacing the forest outside Laylee's home—hoping to be useful in the case that anyone should need him. It was *he* who'd arranged the perfect coincidence by throwing a rock at Laylee's window and alerting Alice to her father's presence.

Alice had rushed to the window to discover Father and Benyamin at exactly the same time; and though an inherent wisdom warned her against acknowledging her young friend aloud, she met his eyes and pressed a finger to her lips, disappearing back inside the castle as she thought quickly of what to do. In the madness and chaos that soon followed, Alice managed to sneak outside just long enough to grab Benyamin's arm and whisper, *"You can travel to Ferenwood by water. Please come find us."*

Benyamin, understanding her meaning at once, handed over his foremost sentinel, Haftpa, without a word of explanation. It was an implicit act of trust that only she and the spider would understand.

"I'll see you soon," Benyamin had said.

And now here she was, running through the forest, Haftpa tucked behind her ear, and Alice could only hope that she and Benyamin would find each other safely. Alice had run without thinking, knowing only that she needed to get far, far away from home, and fast—and it was only once she found herself standing in a patch of forest she hardly recognized that she finally stopped. Breathing hard, chest heaving, she leaned against a tree and said, "What now, Haftpa?"

Just then, a bird swooped down to meet her.

It was big and beautiful, with violet plumage that glittered in the sunlight. Alice had known that Haftpa could talk to other creatures, and she wondered, as the spider clicked its pincers quietly against her ear, whether he was communicating now with this bird. She didn't have to wonder long. The bird cawed and snapped its beak in response to a silent summons and suddenly, without warning, launched upward, snatched Alice in its talons, and soared effortlessly into the sky.

Oliver Newbanks was released with no warning and fell to the ground with a resounding *thump,* jerking in every direction as he tried to free himself from the very strong spider silk strapped across his mouth and joints. He'd fallen flat on his stomach, his face buried in the grass, so when he felt the cold edge of a knife against his skin, he had no way of knowing whether friend or foe was upon him.

But he should have guessed.

Alice Alexis Queensmeadow cut Oliver free and helped him to his feet. Oliver was understandably shaken, and it took him a minute to find his head and figure out what was happening. It was only when he saw Benyamin standing a few feet away that he finally pieced it all together.

"Hi, Oliver." Alice waved the pocketknife, apologizing with her eyes for all the trouble.

And as Oliver waved back—his eyes assessing her uninjured body, her calm demeanor—something occurred to him. "Hey!"

Oliver shouted, turning on Benyamin. "Why didn't you have your spiders tie *her* up? Why just me?"

Benyamin looked surprised. "Well," he said. "It was a group decision, actually. And we didn't think you'd come willingly."

"What?" said Oliver, equally surprised. "Why not?"

"You just . . . you seemed so upset with me," Alice said quietly, stepping forward. "You wouldn't talk to me on the way home. You wouldn't say a word when we got here. You didn't even say good-bye when you left—"

"I waved."

"And I thought—I thought you might hate me for what I'd done."

"Hate you?" Oliver said. "No—Alice, I don't . . ." He trailed off with a sigh, running a shaky hand through his silver hair. "You're my best friend," he said finally. "I don't hate you."

"But you won't even look at me."

Oliver swallowed hard.

"I'm so sorry," Alice said, her voice tinny and small. "You have no idea how sorry I am. Not just for hurting Laylee—but for hurting *you*. I can see how much you care for her."

Oliver looked up, then. Startled.

"Oh, you can't possibly be surprised," said Benyamin, rolling his eyes. "Your infatuation is obvious to everyone."

Oliver flushed a highly unflattering, blotchy sort of red. "You don't"—he cleared his throat—"you don't think it's obvious to her, though, do you?"

Benyamin looked like he might laugh. "I think she's been a bit preoccupied."

"Right," said Oliver, nodding, almost exhaling the word.

"Anyhow." Alice clapped her hands together to gather their attentions. "My point here is that we're going to make this right for Laylee. Benyamin is here to take us back."

"Really?" Oliver looked around, stunned. "How? Actually, wait—how did you get *here*?"

And Benyamin smiled.

❖

They were standing at the edge of a tall cliff in a very remote part of town. There was nothing here but dense vegetation, canopied trees, and tall flowers touching their knees. This was an uninhabited part of Ferenwood for the simple reason that it was a dangerous area to occupy. There was no barrier against the steep fall—plans were still in the works to develop the area—and there were signs posted everywhere warning trespassers away from the edge. Here, the water lashed fast and heavy against the side of the cliff; this exit would be very different from the gentle entry they'd made just that morning. The underwater elevator they'd taken with Father had deposited them in much calmer waters right near the center of town. But this—well, Oliver wasn't sure how they'd survive the jump. The drop was at least a thousand feet.

Most worrisome, however, was the shape of Alice's plan.

She and Benyamin had sketched out their ideas in a few blunt sentences, but Oliver had remained wary. "I still don't understand how you showing up to the courthouse and painting a picture is going to save her job," he'd said to Alice. "How could that possibly be enough?"

"It's not a picture, Oliver," Alice said for what felt like the umpteenth time. "It'll be a *live painting.*"

"But—"

"Don't worry, I've brought my brushes and everything. Father has been teaching me how to focus and refine the colors as I imagine them."

Oliver sighed. "Yes," he said, "I know, and I'm happy you've made progress, but I just—well, our plan is to help Laylee remain a mordeshoor, yes?"

Alice nodded.

"So then isn't my type of magic better suited for the situation? Couldn't I just use my words against them? Say something to convince them?"

This time, it was Benyamin who shook his head. "The effect of your magic is temporary. You'd have to re-convince every member of the jury on a daily basis for the rest of your life. No, no, we need a real, permanent solution." Benyamin began pacing. "Alice painting a living picture of what it is, exactly, that Laylee does could be what changes everything. The people of Whichwood, you see, have no idea what Laylee does for the dead. There are some rumors, of course; a few old wives' tales; but our people haven't the faintest clue how complex, tender, or taxing her work is—or how many steps are involved."

"How is that possible?" said Oliver, stunned. "She's a key member of your society. Her work is invaluable to the revolving door of *existence*."

"Well, it's quite simple, really: They're not supposed to know." Benyamin shrugged. "Laylee's magic is performed exclusively for the dead, and her home is protected by ancient mordeshoor magic that insulates her from the world. Unless there to help her work, a civilian cannot remain for the duration. Of course, volunteers are certainly welcome in the home of a mordeshoor, but as you well know, they're hard to find. So the people are happily ignorant of her suffering."

"Right," said Alice. She took a deep breath. "So. Our plan is to make a case for Laylee's job by showing the people of Whichwood exactly what she does. We want them to know how much she cares—that she has lovingly transported the bodies of their loved ones to the Otherwhere and that no cold, modern magic would honor the deceased the way a mordeshoor does."

"Exactly," said Benyamin, who was beaming at Alice. "If we cannot appeal to their minds, we must appeal to their hearts."

Alice smiled at him as she tugged three large paintbrushes out of her backpack and said, "So I will paint them a beautiful story. Benyamin will narrate."

"And what am I supposed to do?" said Oliver, who'd crossed his arms.

"You," said Alice, "will have to persuade them to sit through it."

❖

Now the insect boy was looking them both up and down. "Ready to get going?"

"Wait," said Oliver, turning to Alice. "Does your father know you're gone?"

Alice shook her head, looking nervous for the first time. "I snuck out. But as long as I can fix this, I know he'll forgive me when I come home."

Oliver could read the determination in her eyes. He knew Alice well enough to know that she would not be dissuaded. "Alright," he said.

Alice nodded. "Let's go."

Benyamin gave her a short bow. When he next lifted his head, he placed two fingers in his mouth and whistled, loud and long. Not moments later, the birds were back.

Cawing as they came, three large purple birds grabbed Alice, Oliver, and Benyamin by the scruffs of their necks, scraping them up into the sky like they might be midnight snacks. The birds circled the open water for only a few seconds before the seas were punctured open by a sudden, violent exhalation of air, followed closely by a glossy body so large the children could only imagine its size.

Oliver heard Alice gasp as the whale yawned open its enormous mouth and, one by one, the birds tossed them inside.

✤

It should be noted here that whales are not generally fast creatures. They are not slow, no, but they are much slower than, say, any kind of train or underwater elevator, to be sure. And in any other scenario, having a very large, rather slow whale as a main source of transportation (whilst in a hurry) might not have seemed like such a coup. But it had taken Benyamin only two hours to get to Ferenwood by whale (let us remember that even the newer, faster underwater contraption had taken two *days*), and here is why:

The magical members of the underwater community (about whom our brave protagonists would one day learn) had used their gifts to build faster paths and tunnels to various parts of the world. These paths were accessible to all native sea dwellers—including animals, magical and non-magical alike. Our age and perspective allows us the privilege of knowing this information now, but it was without understanding how, exactly, this magic worked that Benyamin had learned from his mother that he'd be able to bring his friends back to Whichwood in a timely manner.

In any case, I'm afraid this explanation is interesting only to us; Alice and Oliver were far too pleased and/or distracted to ask any follow-up questions about the commute—they were only happy to be given a second chance to set things right.

NOW,
WHERE
WERE WE?

Laylee wandered the empty, echoing castle halls in a daze.

Dust danced, suspended in strokes of light as she paced up and down carpeted corridors, scenes from the day blurring through ancient, stained-glass windows pockmarking the walls. She could hear the gurgles of a newborn river, fresh snow melting steadily in the afternoon sun, and she paused to listen, her heart racing as she realized how very alone she was. Funny, she had felt lonely for so long now, but she had never been truly alone until now. She looked down at her hands, healthy and brown; touched her cheeks, supple and warm; and counted on six fingers how much she'd lost in her quest to live:

Two parents—

Three friends—

One job—

Laylee no longer knew what to do.

She would go on trial in exactly nineteen hours and had been placed under house arrest until the hour she was required. At precisely nine o'clock tomorrow morning, she would be met at home, shackled, and escorted to the courthouse. Until then, she was physically bound by strict magical reinforcements that imprisoned her within her own walls. Worse still, she wouldn't even be allowed to work. The Elders had forbade any citizen from sending their dead her way; instead, the town would be holding any recently deceased in a secure chamber until her fate was decided; only then (in the event that she should be found guilty) would they enact new measures to deal with the corpses. It seemed a logical enough plan for managing the particulars of her unique situation, but Laylee had already begun to worry.

In the last three days alone, six people had died, and Laylee somehow knew this to be true.

She could feel this truth without the words to articulate why, but when a spirit separated from its body, the specter seemed to sing to her. She'd never before been held away from her spirits, so the sensation was new, but she could feel them—each phantom like a phantom limb, a second heart-beat thudding against her chest. She could practically reach out and curl her fingers around the feeling, knowing without understanding that the dead were calling to her, pushing pain-fully against the magic that repelled their substance from her home. She hadn't known the moment when things changed for her—when it was, exactly, that she'd begun to love her ghosts despite their meanness and mischief, but she knew herself to be their caretaker, and despite her many grumbles about her work, she'd always understood that they needed her—cared for her, even—in the short time they spent together.

Oh, how she missed them now.

It had been a great leniency from the Elders that had allowed Laylee to stay in her own home until the hour of the trial, and she was quietly grateful for it, as she did not think she would do well in a prison cell. And though she hated the people of Whichwood for what they'd done to her father—and for how they'd treated her—Laylee could not imagine herself as anything but a mordeshoor; she knew she had to fight for her right to be the bearer of the dead.

But how? What would she say?

She felt limp, hollowed out, no longer fueled by any kind of passion. She had grieved, yes—she had attempted to empty her heart of its agony—but though she still carried a great deal of pain, she was surprised to find that she felt no violent outrage over the loss of her father or the actions of her people. She felt no desperate madness that would bolster her in court tomorrow. No, Laylee was comforted now by a clarity that helped her understand that Baba never would've returned home to her, that perhaps on his quest for Death he'd been unwittingly searching for a reprieve from life. She knew how much happier he was to have crossed over with Maman—and knowing that Baba was at peace had made her anger a superfluous emotion. She would not begrudge her parents their happiness, so she had to let them go.

She'd let everything go.

She'd been stripped of family, friends, and even her livelihood—but she hadn't expected to be stripped of her anger, too.

A peculiar calm had come over her lately, and it felt a bit like what she'd heard of humility. At every moment she felt a steady, kneading pressure against the back of her neck reminding her that—no matter how bad things were—they could be worse. *Bite your tongue,* said the voice, *and be grateful for what you have lest you lose that, too.*

This was all it took for her to be reminded, in a sudden moment, of Benyamin Felankasak.

Laylee had always thought of Benyamin as simple and weak; she'd considered his kindness a sign of weakness—a symptom of an easy, untroubled life. But after getting to know him and his mother, Laylee wondered if she'd been wrong.

The thing was, Laylee had always resented the smiles of others, their easy charity, their willingness to be kind. But she was beginning to wonder whether she'd gotten her theories confused. Maybe it was not naiveté, but suffering, that inspired kindness. Maybe, she thought, it was pain that inspired compassion.

Just then, she heard her doorbell ring.

❖

Laylee took her time.

She feared the Elders had come for her early—that they'd changed their minds about letting her stay at home—so she moved in slow motion as she tied her long, chestnut locks into a low bun at the base of her neck. She moved even more slowly when the bell rang for the second time, her nervous hands reaching for her fringed, floral scarf from its hook by the door. Carefully, she tied the scarf in an elegant knot at her throat, and calmly, very calmly, she took a deep, steadying breath, and unlocked the door.

Shock rearranged the features on her face.

Benyamin, Oliver, and Alice were waiting for her, and Laylee could not hide the flood of emotions that rushed through her all at once. Happiness, relief, confusion—

Laylee could not have been more surprised.

She'd thought her friends had left her for good. She thought they'd tired of her cold anger and churlish behavior and she couldn't imagine their reasons for returning here, to her home where she'd treated them with nothing but thinly veiled hostility.

"What are you doing here?" Laylee finally spoke, stunned.

"We had to find you," said Oliver too quickly, tripping over his words. He wondered then if she had any idea what she'd done to his brain. "We had to find a way—"

"Find me?" she said, turning to face him fully. She could hardly dare to believe they'd come back just for her. "Why did you want to find me?"

"Well, we came to help you, of course," said a smiling Alice, who was reminded, in a moment of wistfulness, of an identical exchange they'd shared not several nights ago.

But this time, the mordeshoor returned her kindness.

Laylee's face thawed and broke open, the parted lines of her mouth blossoming into a smile that touched her wide, amber eyes. Oliver had never seen Laylee's teeth before—she'd never shown so much emotion—and he spent far too long admiring her mouth in those first moments of their reunion. Laylee didn't seem to mind.

"Actually," said Benyamin quietly, speaking for the first time, "we were wondering if we could come inside for a cup of tea."

I feel I should mention something.

This was not the first time Alice, Oliver, and Benyamin had seen Laylee that day. No—they'd arrived in Whichwood right around noon—and it was now many hours later. The sun was sideways in the sky and the clouds were quickly purpling and the group of them had just returned from a brief gathering at Benyamin's house, where they'd assembled after stumbling upon the mordeshoor during a very private moment. Collectively, they'd decided to leave and never breathe a word about it, but one day Oliver's romantic intentions would encourage him to make the mistake of sharing this story with Laylee. He'd describe what he'd seen and what this moment (and many other moments) had done to him—in hopes of illustrating how he'd come to care for her. Unfortunately, Laylee was horrified to hear it. Which was, of course, how I'd come to hear of it.

This was how they'd discovered her:

It's midday. The sun is directly overhead, happily oblivious to the heavy, ceaseless snowfall blanketing the immense acreage of the mordeshoor's land in a thick, fresh layer of powder. There's a single porcelain tub half submerged in the snow, its depths full to the hilt with scarlet liquid. Within the tub lies our heroine. She is fully clothed, one leg flung over the side of the tub, her head held back, face up to the sky, long brown hair grazing the frost. Her gown is bunched up over one knee and dragging along the edge of the tub, where the sopping lengths of silk drip red water in terrifying patterns over the infant snow. She holds a long bristled brush in one hand and scrubs it roughly against her heavily embellished shoulder; diamonds burst free from their embroidered seams only to land, glittering, in the drift. She appears to be bathing in a pool of her own blood, errant rose petals caught in her hair, crimson tears frozen on her cheeks, and she smiles at something the reader cannot see—a memory?—as she sings softly to the afternoon wind. She sings in a language we cannot understand—something old and beautiful that vibrates on the tongue. It sounds like poetry, like melancholy and sadness. It's Rumi again, her old friend, reminding her of something that soothes her heart.

Here is a translation of the part she sang most clearly:

Don't turn your head
Don't look away from the pain
The wound is the place
Where the light enters you

Mordeshoors were required to be rid of any hypocrisies while washing the dead—which meant they themselves had to be clean in order to properly cleanse. It was a ceremonial washing of the spirit, not the skin, that mattered most, of course, and Laylee had performed these rituals of the mordeshoor with regularity. But on this, the day that might've been her last as a mordeshoor, she was feeling rather emotional about it—and Rumi's words were the only ones that felt quite right for the moment.

And so these were the words they heard when they first saw her, when Oliver and Alice and Benyamin came upon the mordeshoor without meaning to. They'd rung the doorbell several times to no avail, and finally, worried, they'd decided to sneak into the backyard. It was there that they'd discovered this unusual sight; indeed, it was a moment so simultaneously beautiful and disturbing they scarcely knew what to do. (Strange, these were the same two adjectives Alice would one day use to describe her dearest friend to me.) Alice, you see, was in awe; Benyamin was intrigued; but Oliver Newbanks had gone weak in the knees. He reached out without meaning to, grabbing hold of Benyamin's shoulder at first sight of her. Everything about Laylee was unusual and extraordinary— and yet she seemed uninterested in being remarkable in any way. Oliver, who had worked hard his whole life to stand out— to make a mark memorable enough to distinguish him from his peers—could not make sense of this girl, this mordeshoor who did not seem to know or even care whether she terrified or enchanted the world.

But Laylee Layla Fenjoon was in possession of a rare gift she'd yet to understand:

She did not allow the opinions of others to dictate who she was.

This was not a quality she'd been born with. It was not a skill she'd intended to acquire. No, this was an ability forged exclusively from hardship; it was a lesson unearthed from the ashes of betrayal and loss. Pain had hardened her skin while suffering had softened her heart. She was emotion and armor all at once, empathy and resilience combining to create the most intimidating opponent of all.

Still, she wondered then whether she even knew what she was fighting for.

Reader, I share this anecdote of Laylee's bath because I think her time spent therein was transformative. Laylee was assaulted by a barrage of thoughts and feelings as she sat in her porcelain tub that day, and she wondered, with increasing anxiety, what on earth she'd say to a jury to convince them of her worthiness. Most of all, she hated that she had to care what anyone thought of her. She didn't want to change who she was—she didn't want to have to apologize for things she didn't regret—and she worried that Whichwood would want her to alter the composition of her character in order to accommodate their narrow opinions of what was right.

Much later, towel-dried and furnished with a fresh set of clothes, Laylee would hear the doorbell ring for the first time. She would descend the wheezing staircase of her ancient home with a tightening apprehension, feeling desperately alone and outnumbered. She had no expectations—no certainty of anything but disappointment—and yet, as she reached into her pocket to curl a loose fist around her father's twenty-six remaining teeth, she dared to hope for a miracle.

Clever reader, I wonder—is the end of our story coming into focus for you?

Do you require the many details of the next twenty-four hours to know whether our mordeshoor's tale ends in triumph or heartbreak? It is my dearest wish to skip ahead and simply tell you what happened, but I fear you might require more than a mere summary. Where should we begin?

Would it be of interest to you to know what the children discussed that evening? To know that they gathered round Laylee's humble fire with cups of hot tea while Alice excitedly shared her plan to save Laylee's career?

Or perhaps you'd like to hear more about how Laylee laughed until she cried, falling backward onto a dusty chair as Benyamin and Oliver bickered over the details of who, exactly, would be playing a more critical role in saving the day tomorrow?

Alice and Benyamin and Oliver were all so certain of their imminent success that Laylee couldn't bring herself to poke holes in their happiness. Besides, she was tired of being cynical; tonight Laylee would keep her worries to herself and, for the first time in a long time, allow herself to act her age. The three friends had been carrying an unwieldy stack of presents when they'd appeared at her door, and Laylee now sat in front of the fire, smiled a brilliant smile at her friends, and began to open the brightly wrapped *cadeaux*. The gifts were the handiwork of Benyamin's mother, who believed with every bit of her heart that a few home-cooked treats could heal even the harshest wounds.

Reader, Benyamin's mother was rarely wrong.

These last few days Laylee had been subsisting on eggplant soup and a few overripe beets, and so it was with a pure, child-like glee that she ripped open her presents, gasping aloud as she unearthed tins of buttery pistachio brittle; slim strips of chewy, rose-petal nougat; and clear mason jars packed with pomegranate seeds. She nearly cried over the diamonds of cardamom pudding and their daintily slivered almonds; she jumped to her feet as she uncovered the dishes of warm, creamy halva with their flourishes of cinnamon; she very nearly lost her mind over the boxes of cakes, fresh cream puffs, and Persian baklava. She'd already been fighting back tears when Benyamin pointed out that she'd yet to see the bowls of slippery glass noodles (sweetened with rosewater) and the large tubs of saffron ice cream.

Laylee had been rendered speechless.

It was a veritable feast unlike any she'd ever enjoyed, and she was so overwhelmed by the gesture—so very overcome by the company—that she couldn't help stumbling as she tried to say thank you.

Laylee, Alice, Benyamin, and Oliver camped out in her living room that night. They needn't worry about any wayward spirits now that Laylee's home had been magically sterilized for ghosts, and they stayed up until dawn drinking tea, telling stories, and discussing the many details of nothing and everything. Their conversations were interrupted only by pauses to stuff their mouths with buttery candies and creamy ice cream, and finally, after the clocks themselves grew tired of ticking, Laylee fell into a deep, heavenly sleep and dreamed of a world where she would always have her friends by her side.

The thing that no one had been expecting, of course, was that the ghosts would get loose again.

There were only six of them this time, but, as I mentioned some pages ago, it had been a very long time since anyone had respected mordeshoors, so even the Elders had underestimated the power of Laylee's magic. The moment she was hauled by her handcuffs through the doors of the city courthouse, the spirits could no longer be contained. Laylee was now closer than she'd ever been to these fresh phantoms, and sensing her nearness, they were bolstered by a connection far more powerful than the simple magical bind the Elders had used to subdue them.

And so it was amid a sudden, disturbing rush of noise, exclamation, riot, and chaos, that Whichwood's town magistrate attempted to call their day into order. The problem was, no one could understand what was happening. Luckily, the ghosts were still too fresh to be interested in stealing skins just yet, but their newness to the world meant that they were only interested in making trouble. Young ghosts (no matter their human age) were preoccupied only by the need to make a fuss when they first arrive. It's a fairly intolerable period—one that Laylee never cared for—but now, as she sat in her seat and watched the spirits wreak havoc upon the composures of the most esteemed members of her community, she had to fight back a smile. Ghosts rushed by, upending stacks of paperwork, blowing out all the lanterns, and knocking over ladies' hats. They spun around Laylee's head, shouting any number of things at her—

"Mordeshoor! Mordeshoor!" This, from a tiny little girl. "Can we please go home now?"

"I don't like it here at all," said a curly-haired woman who'd just knocked over a samovar.

"Neither do I," said an elderly gentleman who was trying and failing to pull down people's trousers. "Why are we here? Why don't we leave, Mordeshoor?"

Laylee sent them pleading looks and pressed a single finger to her lips, hoping they would calm down.

"Ooooooh," said a pimply teenage boy, "I think she's in trouble."

"What do you mean, *in trouble*?" said the tiny girl. She flew up to the ceiling and sat upside down. "How can a mordeshoor be in trouble?"

Just then, one of the older ghosts rattled a window so hard it

shattered; splintered glass rained into the room, eliciting startled cries and screams from the jury. No one seemed able to
make sense of the nonsense, and Laylee was surprised by their
ignorance. But Laylee knew she'd be found out eventually, and
she figured she'd better get these ghosts in line before they ruined her chances today. She could've easily said something to
them. She felt her fingers twitch as they reached for the whip
that hung from the tool belt she wore around her waist.

Still, she hesitated.

For so long, this had been Laylee's greatest secret: that she
could see and speak with the ghosts. She'd always worried that
outing herself as a direct liaison between human and spirit
would only make her job more burdensome; she worried the
people would pester her for communications from the dead, for
last words from their loved ones—and she'd wanted nothing to
do with it. But now she wondered whether it was still a secret
worth keeping. Wouldn't it lend credibility to her profession if
her people knew she could actually see the spirit emerge as the
body failed? Could this not help her, somehow?

She hadn't finished thinking it all through before the silence was interrupted again. Alice, Benyamin, Oliver, and
Madarjoon had pushed through the front doors of the courtroom with great fanfare, making no effort to hide their presence. Her friends had needed to take a separate train into
town to catch the proceedings but, after elbowing their way

through the mass of people crowding the exterior doors, Oliver had easily persuaded their way into the main hall and secured their seats up front. In fact, they were just settling into said seats when one of Laylee's ghosts blew a gust of wind so strong it knocked the wig off the magistrate's head. Furious, he slammed his gavel down several times, shouting for someone to fetch his hair from the floor and then, impossibly angrier, he pointed one sausage-y finger at Laylee and demanded she explain herself. *She* was somehow causing all this commotion, he said, and he didn't know why or how, but he simply knew it to be true, and if she didn't stop this nonsense right this instant, he would throw the entire case out and sentence her himself.

Laylee blanched.

"What does he mean, Mordeshoor?" asked a twentysomething-year-old. He'd stopped in the middle of an attempt to push over a table. "Why did he say he would sentence you? For what?"

"What's going on?" said the tiny girl, who was beginning to cry. She stomped her feet along the ceiling so hard the entire room began to shake. "Why can't we go home?"

"YOUNG LADY," said the magistrate. "Did you hear what I said? If you don't stop this right now, I'll pass through a judgment to dissolve your mordeshoor magic *immediately*—"

"What—no!" cried the curly-haired woman, spinning circles around the angry judge.

"This is an outrage!" The elderly gentleman whooshed up to Laylee's face so fast she had to sit back in her chair. "What would we do without a mordeshoor?"

Please, Laylee begged them again with her eyes, but her ghosts wouldn't take the hint. The teenage spirit began shouting obscenities and rattling the remaining windows and the magistrate went so red in the face that Laylee was sure everything was about to fall apart. Desperate, she turned to her friends in a sudden panic, and in the time it took her to spin around, Oliver had already handled the situation. Not a moment later, the magistrate was sitting calmly in his seat, reading slowly from an official document. Laylee visibly exhaled.

She would find a way to deal with the ghosts later—for now, things needed to go according to the original plan.

The first half of the day dragged on.

Oliver administered persuasion where necessary in dealing with outbursts from the ghosts, while the counsel representing the interests of "The People of Whichwood" put forth what seemed like an endless stream of withering arguments against Laylee and the legacy of the mordeshoor. The ghosts, who were listening closely the whole time, were only growing more hostile. Their outbursts grew more violent as the day wore on, and it was all Laylee could do to keep from flinching at their angry cries, spontaneous tears, and rage-induced epithets. It was hard enough trying to ignore her ghosts' fuming—

"Who do they think they are," said the curly-haired lady, "telling our mordeshoor she can't do her job?" She flew past a set of doors so aggressively they nearly came off their hinges.

"Threatening to take away her magic—"

"We can never let that happen!"

"They propose using those vile, modern methods," said

the older-gentleman ghost, "as if there's any replacement for a mordeshoor! Modern magic would just throw us in the ground!"

"There's no decency in it!"

But it was even harder for Laylee to sit through the accusations of incompetence from the prosecution. The arguments against her were so effortlessly dismissive—

"She's just a child who has no idea what she's doing!"

"She should be playing with dolls, not dead people!"

—that Laylee found it hard to imagine anyone would disagree. Every time one of the solicitors would shout some flippant nonsense about the obvious need to "put this infant on a playground, not a cemetery," the jury nodded their heads in eager assent. Laylee looked away, heartbroken.

In the end, the mordeshoor was left feeling terribly demoralized.

The prosecution comprised seven attorneys, all angry and impassioned. On Laylee's side, however, it was just her and a young, uninspired lawyer who'd been assigned to her that very morning. Meanwhile, the robust prosecution had presented hours of painful, genuinely thoughtful rhetoric compounded by another hour of rigorous questioning that succeeded in making Laylee feel small and inconsequential.

From the transcript:

"Do you go to school, young lady?"

"No."

"Do you have any toys?"

"No."

"Is that blood on your clothes?"

"I—yes, but—"

"Do you have any parents?"

Silence.

From the judge: "Please answer the question, Ms.
 Fenjoon."

"No," said Laylee quietly. "I do not have any parents."

"So you live alone?"

"Yes."

"In an old, drafty castle, where you spend your days
 by yourself washing the bodies of dead pe—"

From the defense: "Objection, Your Honor—what is
 the point here?"

From the judge: "Overruled. I'd like to see where this
 is going."

Back to the prosecution: "Let me put it like this:
 Wouldn't you *like* to go to school?"

"Yes."

"Wouldn't you *like* to have toys and clean clothes and
 live with a family who loved you and took care of

you so you could enjoy your childhood instead of
having to work so hard?"

Laylee hesitated, feeling her throat close up. "Well,"
she said quietly. "I—I'd—"

From the judge: "The question, Ms. Fenjoon. Answer
the question. And remember that you are under
oath."

"Yes," Laylee whispered, feeling like she might cry,
and hung her head in shame.

"I have no further questions, Your Honor."

What Laylee didn't know how to say was this: She wanted it
all. She wanted to go to school and have a family and enjoy her
childhood and *still* get to be a mordeshoor. She didn't want to
lose this part of her life.

She just wanted more.

I must tell you straightaway: Alice's plan worked well. It did not, however, work as well as she had hoped.

❖

The second half of the day was beautifully dramatic. As soon as Laylee's side was offered a chance to present their defense, Oliver made Laylee's young attorney sit down, cease speaking, and focused the attentions of every person present. The stage was set for Alice.

Our talented friend from Ferenwood did not disappoint. She began by extinguishing all the light and color from the room, turning the entire space into a black backdrop upon which she would tell a story. Paintbrushes clutched in one hand, she nodded at Benyamin, ready to follow his lead as he narrated, step by step, the many intricate details involved in washing the dead. It was the only time during the entire day that the ghosts actually sat quietly and listened; they were heartened not only by the story, but by the pictures Alice had painted.

Alice's illustrations were so lifelike they startled even her; she'd only ever done this sort of thing in private, on a much smaller scale—but her ability was proving to be even more impressive than she first suspected. Her talent was such that she could easily impress infinite colors (hence: images) from her own mind onto any canvas. She could manipulate pigment in any way she wanted with the simple wish of her mind, and her brushes helped her focus the size, scope, and placement of the images. It was a long demonstration, the details of which I will not burden you with (as you, dear reader, already know exactly how Laylee washes her dead), but I will tell you this: Alice painted the story with all the skill of a seasoned artist, and Benyamin, whose narration was intentionally affecting, seemed to be hitting each emotional beat with aplomb—though no part of his presentation was more impressive than when he described the tens of thousands of eternally red roses Laylee had planted in honor of each spirit. At this part in the story, the ghosts actually burst into tears, sobbing so loudly Laylee had to strain to hear Benyamin's voice. The six specters huddled around their mordeshoor and whispered words of encouragement, promising her that no matter what happened today, they would never abandon her. Laylee was moved despite herself, and couldn't fight the tears that sprung to her eyes.

Along the way, Oliver did quick and clever magic that encouraged all people present to accept this unusual show as a solid (and ordinary) defense for Laylee's position and, by the time it was over, the room had fallen into a thoughtful, careful silence that slowly—then quickly—grew into a roar of anxious whispers. The magistrate had to bang his gavel to get the room in order.

Laylee looked at the jury with a nervous sort of anticipation, scanning their eyes for any indication that they may have been moved by Alice's story. Sadly, their faces were inscrutable. Laylee felt her heart sink.

The judge nodded at Laylee's attorney. "Would you like to call any witnesses to the stand?"

"No, Your Hono—"

"Yes!" said Laylee, who stood upright with such suddenness she surprised herself.

Laylee's attorney blinked at her. He had the face of a field mouse.

"Your Honor," she said more steadily, "that is—I would like to testify."

❖

Her friends had fought so hard for her today—and for their help and their stubborn affection she would be eternally grateful—but now it was time for her to fight for herself. The prosecution had made her feel weak and juvenile, two things she knew she wasn't. They'd called her actions irresponsible and flighty—citing these characteristics as symptoms intrinsic to her youth. They'd pressed at her age like it was something to be ashamed of, using the word *child* as a pejorative term and impressing upon the jury the idea that she was, as a consequence of her few years on this planet, an ineffectual human being, an incompetent creature devoid of passion or intention and, ultimately, incapable of thinking for herself.

None of this was true.

Laylee was thirteen years old, yes, but she had lived, she had loved, she had suffered—and her age was no reason for her feelings to be so easily and carelessly diminished. She was not lesser for being younger; her hurts were no less important; her feelings no less relevant. These were the things she said that day—chin up, shoulders back—even as she felt something shattering inside of her. She was all alone in the world now, and save the kindness of her new friends, she had no one upon whom she might rely except herself.

Surely, she said, that was enough to earn her the respect of her elders?

(Here, her ghosts cheered, eagerly knocking lanterns off the walls.)

Instead of taking away what was important to her, shouldn't they stop the people from taking advantage of her? Laylee had been abused and manipulated from the moment she began her life as an independent mordeshoor. The inherent bias against her youth and her gender and her consequent inability to be taken seriously in a society that belittled her—*this* was what had led to the collapse of their system. It was not that she was incapable. It was that she had been overworked and under-valued. It was that she deserved more respect than she was allotted.

And she would no longer sit idly by as they denigrated her character.

"Are you quite finished, Ms. Fenjoon?" said the magistrate.

Laylee hesitated.

"Ms. Fenjoon?"

"Tell him I never liked him," shouted the curly-haired ghost. "My stupid cousin. I died yesterday and he didn't even care enough to take today off."

Laylee's eyebrows shot up her face. She turned to look at the curly-haired ghost.

"Ms. Fenjoon," the magistrate said again, "if you're finished, please—"

"No," Laylee said suddenly. Her heart was racing. She could tell that she was losing this battle—Alice's presentation hadn't worked as well as they'd hoped, and her own words appeared to be worthless to this angry old man. She really felt she had no choice anymore.

The magistrate sighed as he checked the time on the wall. "What else do you wish to say?"

"I—that is"—she cleared her throat—"Your Honor, with all due respect, your cousin wishes me to tell you that—"

"Tell him he's a perfectly useless dingbat!"

"—that she's, um, unhappy you chose to come in to work today." And then, more quickly, "Despite the fact that she died yesterday."

The magistrate's hand hovered over his gavel, his face frozen between several emotions.

"My cousin?" he said finally, blinking fast.

"Yes," Laylee said nervously. "She's about medium height, curly red hair—"

Cheerfully, the ghost said, "My name is Zari."

"And—and her name is Zari," Laylee finished rather lamely. She'd never done this before—this communicating between the living and the dead—and she realized she was very bad at it.

"How—how do you know this—"

"She's standing right in front of me," Laylee said. "Your cousin's ghost has been bouncing around the courthouse all day today. It was she who knocked the wig off your head earlier."

A juror stood up at once, visibly shaking. "You can see them?" she said. "You can see the dead? You can communicate with them?"

"Yes," said Laylee. "It's an inherent part of my magic as a mordeshoor. I can exist in both worlds."

A sudden, series of gasps inhaled the room.

And then—

Chaos.

"Why has she never mentioned this before?"

"What if she's lying?"

"Impossible, though, really, impossible—"

"She could've learned about your cousin from anyone!"

"She's manipulating your emotions, Your Honor!"

"What are the odds—"

"How dare you lie about something like this, young lady—"

"—but to overturn a magic like this? Communicating with the unseen world?"

"The consequences could be grave—"

"I still say she's too young!"

"It's too dangerous to meddle—"

"What else does she know?"

"How cruel to keep such a secret!"

"And a child, really—only a child—"

"SILENCE!"

The magistrate stood and slammed his gavel, bellowing the command several times before the room settled into a tense, electric sort of quiet.

Laylee's heart would not cease its kicking. She felt her hands shaking in her lap and she curled them into fists. She had no idea what she'd unleashed—what kind of consequences she would suffer for her admission—and she felt something like fear catch in her throat.

The magistrate fixed her with an unflinching look for a measure of time that Laylee would later estimate to have lasted about ten minutes. Oliver would clarify that it was only a matter of seconds.

Finally, the judge spoke. "You are a terrible little liar, Ms. Fenjoon. And your deceitfulness will cost you—"

"No, Your Honor, I swear I'm not lying—"

"QUIET!"

Laylee flinched, suddenly so terrified she felt frozen in her seat. This was not how she thought things would turn out.

"You dare to come into my courtroom and lie to me under oath?" the magistrate demanded. "You dare to use the occasion of my cousin's death to manipulate me? To taunt me?" He was shouting now, going purple in the face. "You think I am so easily bullied?" He slammed his gavel down hard.

"N-no, Your Honor—I never—"

"Interrupt me one more time, young lady, and I will have you held in contempt!" The magistrate narrowed his eyes. "Our overdependence on superstition," he said quietly, "has crippled our city. Our weakness of mind has kept us shackled to outmoded, useless institutions. *Yours,*" he said viciously, "in particular. Why do we fear the mordeshoor so much?" He turned to the jury now. "Why do we fear the dead? We are terrified to even visit the graves of our loved ones—why? Because superstition dictates that visiting our dead will only encourage their corpses to come back into our lives. Nonsense!" he cried. "We are governed by *nonsense*. And I will stand for it no longer."

Laylee felt her heart seize.

"Laylee Layla Fenjoon—I find you guilty of all charges. You will be sentenced to six months in prison and stripped of your magic forthwith—"

"But, Your Honor!" cried her useless attorney. "The jury!"

The magistrate hesitated for half a second before turning to the jury. "Respected members of the jury," he said, "all those in favor of sentencing this witch, say aye."

"Aye!" they chorused.

"All those opposed?"

Silence.

"No!" Alice screamed. The pale girl ran forward and Benyamin caught her around the waist, hauling her backward. "Please," she cried, "Your Honor—this is a mistake—"

But the judge had only looked at her with disgust, tossed his gavel to the floor, and walked out.

The courtroom exploded into chaos.

People were shouting all at once and all over each other,

spreading the news (and their unsolicited opinions) like a virus. Laylee, meanwhile, had gone numb. She couldn't see or hear properly anymore. There was a deafening rush of sound reverberating in her eardrums that made it impossible to distinguish voices. She couldn't believe this was happening. Was this really happening? Had she really thought she'd be found guilty? Like this?

She hardly noticed when someone grabbed her roughly by the arm and marched her out of the courtroom, so it was only as she had one foot out the door that she remembered to look back.

Alice was still screaming, kicking furiously as Benyamin, who was white as milk, fought to hold her back from doing something dangerous. Madarjoon looked stricken.

And Oliver Newbanks stood tall and said nothing, silent tears streaming down his face.

It was then that Laylee was struck by a sudden, terrifying idea, the likes of which I must assure you she would never, ever have considered under any other circumstances. But reader, she was desperate. Her ghosts were still hanging about the room, staring at her in shock and dismay, too stunned even to speak, and it was in this moment, overcome by a delirious panic, that she cried out to these creatures, the spirits only she could see, and said, "Tell them I've asked for their return!"

The ghosts did not respond. They merely blinked.

"Tell them!" she cried. "Do you understand? You have to hurry—"

But then, and perhaps most disturbing of all: Her ghosts very abruptly disappeared.

So soon?

Had her magic already been broken? Where would the ghosts go? What would happen to them now?

Laylee was devastated. Sadness blew through her like a sudden gust of wind as she realized, with a final, inward collapse, that she'd no moves left to make. She felt dizzy with resignation, the weight of the day crashing into her so swiftly she could hardly stand.

The next hour was a blur.

Laylee was carted down several hallways by coarse, unsympathetic hands, navigating a serpentine path so complicated it practically guaranteed that even if she broke free, she'd never find her way out. Eventually she was shoved in a holding cell in a back room of the courthouse and left there without a word.

Her mind was whirring. She was going to jail. *Jail.* For six months. No magic. Her breathing was coming in fast and hard in sharp, harsh exhales that began to terrify her. She couldn't catch her breath. She felt the room spin around her. Stumbling to her feet, she ran, without thinking, to the trash can in the corner and heaved the contents of her breakfast into the basket. Her hands were shaking; her bones felt brittle. Her skin was cold and clammy and she made her way slowly to the single, thin bed shoved to one side of the room and somehow convinced her legs to bend as she sat there, waiting for life to crush what was left of her spirit.

It was then that she realized, with the full force of reality behind her, that she'd never expected things to go so badly today. She'd secretly, quietly—desperately—hoped that after all she'd been through, fate would finally lend a hand. She thought she'd finally have a chance at happiness.

She'd dared to dream of a happily ever after.

Instead, she'd been given shackles.

The deputies had returned, metal cuffs clanging in their hands. The two officers chained her wrists and ankles together so tightly the metal cut into her skin, drawing blood, and when she gasped at the pain, she was met only with dark, dirty looks that told her to be quiet.

Laylee fought back a flood of tears with every bit of dignity she had left.

She stood tall as she was forced out of her cell and down a dark corridor, flanked on either side by officers holding on to her far more tightly than was necessary. She held her head high, even as they pushed open doors to the outside, where a mob of journalists and nosy onlookers were waiting like vultures, ready to prey on the injured. Laylee narrowed her eyes as she swallowed back the lump in her throat and only faltered when she saw her friends standing off to the side, holding on to one another for support. The officers yanked Laylee forward through the crowd, shoving reporters out of the way—

"Ms. Fenjoon, will you try to appeal your case?"

"Ms. Fenjoon—Ms. Fenjoon—what do you think your father would say if he were still alive?"

"Ms. Fenjoon—how are you feeling right now?" one lady shouted as she shoved a recorder in Laylee's face. "Do you feel the judgment was fair?"

—and Laylee latched on to the faces of her friends, unblinking, unwilling to break eye contact, as she felt her heart dismantle in her chest.

"Thank you," she whispered, the tears falling fast now. "For everything."

And then it was over. She was shoved into the back of a large, windowless steel carriage, and sat quietly in the corner as the roar of the crowd faded away. This was her life now. And she would learn to accept it.

That is—she *would've* learned to accept it, if the transport she'd been traveling in hadn't been knocked over at precisely that moment. Laylee was flung suddenly to one side, hitting her head hard against the metal. A painful ringing exploded in her ears, and she winced against the sensation as lights flared behind her eyelids.

What was happening?

She was on her knees now, her hands and legs two useless clumps as she struggled to get back on her feet. Then, just as the ringing began to subside, a sudden, violent roar tore open the silence, and a single hand punched a hole through the wall. Laylee screamed. A second hand punched a second hole. And then the two hands ripped open the wall of the carriage as if it were made of paper.

Laylee scuttled further into the darkness of the overturned carriage, not knowing what was happening to her. Was someone here to help her or hurt her? And who on earth could rip through reinforced sheets of metal?

It was only when she heard the sound of the slow, happy voice that Laylee finally understood: The horrors of the day had, happily, only just begun.

"Laylee?" said the gummy, rolling voice. "Laylee *joonam*—"

"Baba?" she said softly. "Is that you?"

"Yes, *azizam*," said her father's corpse. "Your maman and I are here to help."

Reader, they had risen from the dead.

FINALLY,
A BIT OF
GOOD
NEWS

Mordeshoors did not have the power to raise the dead—this was not a magic entrusted to the living. No, only the *dead* could ask their fellow dead to wake, and today it was at Laylee's behest that her six spirits had gone and raised an army. As soon as the request left Laylee's lips, they'd been moved to action immediately, making haste to the castle they knew instinctively to be their new home. These ghosts, you will remember, had made their mordeshoor a promise—they'd vowed to stand by her, no matter the outcome of her trial— and now, having received a direct call to action, they intended to follow through on that promise. There were many tens of thousands of dead bodies planted in Laylee's backyard, and when the ghosts explained to the quietly snoozing earth that Laylee—their resident (and favorite) mordeshoor—had asked for their help, the corpses were more than happy to interrupt their final rest for a quick adventure.

I cannot emphasize this enough: Mordeshoor magic took great care with the dead.

The rituals Laylee performed for the body carried great benefits underground; so much so that even in their coffins, the bodies were cocooned by a softness they could not see. Dead limbs were carefully bandaged in magical protections that would make their journey through the earth more comfortable. It was true that once the spirit had separated from the body it would move on to the Otherwhere, yes, but there was still an echo—a residue of the spirit seared inside the flesh—and this echo would continue to feel things, even after death. Laylee's work was so sensitive to this understanding that even for this remnant spirit she would perform a great kindness, embalming the body in a cool, invisible liquid that made the underground passage more tolerable. It was all a gift, yes, yes, a comfort. But Laylee had not performed this magic with any thought of what it would do to the body should it decide to reanimate. She'd never once considered what it would look like to see such a body emerge from the ground.

Perhaps she should have.

Baba had ripped open Laylee's shackles quite easily, tossing the manacles into the open snow, and helped his daughter climb out of the overturned carriage. And as she stepped into the cold, winnowing winter light, she could see the mass of dead faces staring out at her, tens of thousands of them, each body looking like it'd been dipped in many translucent layers of wax. The effect was such that their figures looked deeply distorted; it was like seeing a person through warped glass, the edges soft where they shouldn't be, eyes clouded, hair matted, noses indistinguishable from cheeks. The sun was beginning its descent and the light shattered across the horizon, errant strokes of light spearing these milky bodies and illuminating further the oddities that distinguished them from their former selves. There was a thick webbing between their fingers and elbows, their teeth had melted into their lips, their knees bent with a strange, metallic clicking sound, and their fingers were without fingernails, having been pulled by the mordeshoor herself.

Even so, Laylee couldn't hide a shudder.

She said nothing for a full minute, stunned and horrified and somehow—deeply, deeply moved. She didn't know what she felt more: pride or terror, and in the end, the only thing she could think to say was this:

"Friends," she said softly. "Thank you so much for coming."

I think it will not surprise you to hear that these excitable corpses soon stormed the city. They stomped through the beautiful, historical center of Whichwood en masse, thousands upon thousands of them marching fearlessly across the cerulean streets of town with one goal:

To leave an impression.

Whichwood had ceased believing in its mordeshoors. Their lack of faith in this tradition had failed them and their town and, in the process, had turned them against an innocent young girl and her father, painting them both with scarlet letters of injustice. Laylee had been starving and hardly surviving for years; she was underpaid, desperately overworked, and treated like a pariah. No one respected her. Strangers dumped their dead on Laylee's doorstep and disappeared, sometimes leaving a token of payment, sometimes leaving nothing at all. She wore ancient rags and slept in the bitter cold, too poor to afford even enough firewood, and still our young protagonist devoted herself to her job—and to the many dead she had loved.

Today, dear reader, they would stand up for her. (Quite, ahem, literally.)

The magic that embalmed the flesh of the dead had made them inhumanly strong—it was this same strength that enabled them to dig their way out of the ground—and it made them formidable opponents. The superstitious Whichwoodians were too terrified to stand against the walking corpses as they tore through town, ripping poles out of the ground and knocking carriages into the sea. The six ghosts were squealing with delight as they flew overhead—but of course the living could not see these spirits, so the terrified expressions of civilians were focused only on the walking wax figures. Laylee, followed closely by Maman and Baba, led the group of them, while Roksana (you remember Roksana, do you not?) walked alongside our mordeshoor, one inhuman hand laid protectively on her shoulder.

Laylee wondered in every moment where her friends might've gone—and whether they were still here—but there was never a chance to stop and find them. Laylee was now in charge of an army, you see, and they required quite a lot of guidance. Our mordeshoor was able to manage things in a general way, but there were so many thousands of corpses following her that it was hard to keep track of those among them that ripped landmarks, streetlamps, food carts, and passenger sleighs from the ground only to fling them into the distance.

Laylee didn't *really* want violence or mayhem—she wanted only her freedom. Was it possible, she wondered, to have the latter without the former?

Laylee didn't know. After all, she'd never been in this position before. And though her parents stood right in front of her—ripe for the asking—she knew that these figures before her were only evaporated versions of the real thing. These were not *people* who were fighting for her; they were *memories* of people wearing milky flesh. And very soon, they had seized the city.

Laylee was ready to leave her mark.

At her direction, a couple thousand corpses had split from the group and made it their mission to collect the many magistrates and Town Elders from their homes and hiding places. Now they were dragging the screaming, writhing bodies of prominent figures into the center square, where the rest of the waxy horde had gathered. It was beyond insanity—it was anarchy.

It was then that Roksana leaned in to her mordeshoor and said, "What would you like us to do to them?"

And Laylee merely smiled.

Screams pierced the silence in steady con-tractions of pain.

The sun had scrambled behind a mountain and the moon peeked out only occasionally from behind a cloud. Birds had hidden in the trees; horses had galloped away—even the crickets knew better than to make a sound tonight. The corpses had been playing with the Town Elders like cats would toy with prey, and Laylee, who was still haunted by images of Baba being murdered before her eyes, would be lying if she said she wasn't enjoying the show. She watched as the dead tossed her town's important men and women into the sky only to catch them again and quickly fling them in the sea. Someone would then fetch their sopping bodies out of the water and sit them in the snow where icicles formed immediately across their skin and then, once they'd nearly frozen, another corpse would come along and punt the shaking figures into a tree, where they'd land with a hard *thump,* and eventually slide roughly down the tall trunk. They'd soon amassed a rather large heap of hurting bodies.

Somewhere in her heart, Laylee knew she shouldn't be dragging things out like this, but she felt suddenly fueled by a righteous anger that demanded retribution against her townspeople. How deeply they'd hurt her. How deeply they'd cut into her heart. They'd spit in her face at every opportunity, hissing as she passed, dismissing her from schools and shops. She was loathed for invented reasons, mistreated for their own profit; she starved and no one cared—and the only parent she had left, they'd killed.

How could she ever forgive them?

At Laylee's command, the entire city—nearly all eighty thousand people—had been dragged out of their homes and forced to bear witness to the activities of the evening. The corpses, who had no interest in anything but serving their mordeshoor, would never question her methods. They would never tell her to show mercy to the people who'd hurt her. And had Laylee no one else upon whom to rely, she might have lost herself to the madness. A sudden influx of power, violent anger, crushing heartbreak, and mass chaos—

Well.

I fear that, with no one else to question her, Laylee might've gone too far.

But it was then that her friends came rushing through the crowd.

Alice and Oliver and Benyamin were breathless and exhausted by the effort of finding her, but they were so thrilled to have been reunited with the mordeshoor that they toppled into one another, pulling Laylee into their arms as they fell. Laylee leaned back to look her friends in the eyes, blinking several times. Her movements were stunned and slow, as if she'd been startled out of a trance.

Madarjoon, Benyamin quickly explained, was safely out of the way of the stampede, but the three of them had been searching for Laylee for hours. They'd only, finally, managed to find her because of Haftpa, who'd been trying to convince the circling ghosts to give up her exact location.

"Well, thank goodness for Haftpa," Laylee said. "I'm so glad you're alright."

"So what are we going to do to stop this?" said Oliver quickly. "I was thinking we—"

"Stop this?" Laylee said, confused. "What do you mean? Stop what?"

All three children looked stunned—and then, scared. For a moment, no one said anything.

"You have to call off the corpses," Benyamin finally said. His eyes were pulled together in concern. "You can't let them keep hurting these people."

"Hurting them?" Laylee said softly, turning to look out on the crowd. She almost laughed. "What they're experiencing now? This hurt? This is nothing compared to what they've put me through."

"But, Laylee—"

"No," Laylee said angrily. "You don't understand. You don't know. *You can't know.*" She swallowed, hard, her voice catching as she spoke. "This pain," she said, pressing one hand against her chest. "You don't know, you don't know." She was nearly crying as she said, "I've lived with their cruelty for so long—"

It was Alice who suddenly stepped forward and said, "You're right. You're absolutely right."

Laylee stopped to stare at her, surprised.

"But they're not worth your time," said Alice. "They're not worth what this will do to you. And I can see that this"— she gestured to the madness—"this is hurting you. You might get your revenge today, but you'll still wake up unhappy tomorrow. There's no relief in this," she said, shaking her head. "Only more suffering. Your suffering."

And Laylee hesitated, turning away as a remembered pain creased her forehead.

"They don't deserve you," Alice said softly, stepping forward to take Laylee's hands in her own. "And you don't need these worthless people to tell you what you're worth."

Laylee looked up, tears falling silently down her cheeks.

"You have us," said Alice. "And we already know you're priceless."

Everything else was fairly easy after that.

Laylee knew she had to call off the corpses. She knew she would ask them to stand down. There was only one problem:

"How will I get their attention all at once?" she said. "There are so many of them—"

Benyamin cleared his throat. "Well," he said, smiling. "Haftpa and his friends can build you a web."

Everyone stared at him.

"In the sky, obviously," Benyamin clarified. "They could weave it between two tall trees, and it'll be big enough, sticky enough, and strong enough to hold you. From up there, you'll be plenty visible."

"Alright," said Laylee slowly. "But how do I get up there?"

"Easy," said Oliver. "We'll get one of the corpses to toss you up."

❖

It took a while to build the complicated contraption, but eventually Laylee would find herself in the very unique position of being caught in an inhumanly large spiderweb, staring out over nearly two hundred thousand people, both dead and alive. It was only after the bizarreness of the moment wore off that she realized it was not enough for her to simply be strung from the sky. No one was noticing her in this darkness—they were all too preoccupied with the cruel Olympics she and her corpses had cultivated.

So she did the only thing she knew how to do:

She unhooked her whip from where it hung on her tool belt and snapped it three times through the air—the sounds like thunderclaps quaking the heavens—and that, it turned out, was enough to gather their attentions. People craned their necks to catch a glimpse of the mordeshoor suspended in a spiderweb, her long leather whip held high in one hand. Once she knew they were looking—listening, even—Laylee felt suddenly at ease. In all the recent mess and mania, she'd forgotten who she was—but of course: She was a mordeshoor.

And she was in charge here.

"Dearest dead friends," she said, her voice ringing out into the night. "You disrupted an important sleep to stand beside me today, and you must know how grateful I am, from the bottom of my heart, for your loyalty and your kindness. But we must end the madness here tonight. There's no need to torture these people any longer. Please," she said, "let them go."

"But, Mordeshoor," said Roksana, "you said you wanted them to apologize, and they haven't apologized yet. They haven't promised to change their ways as you requested—"

"Is that what you want?" cried one of the shivering Town Elders. "You just want us to apologize?"

"She wants you to recognize the error of your ways!" cried Maman. "You can never again disrespect the mordeshoor. Our loyalty is—and always will be—to her and her lineage!"

"Yes! You will repent your ways!" cried a corpse from the crowd.

"You will pay her a decent wage!" shouted another.

"You will never mistreat her again!" the crowd bellowed all together.

"We're so sorry," said a new, nervous voice. It was the magistrate from the morning's proceedings. "We're so very, very sorry"—he was openly sobbing now. "We'll never again make the mistake of denying the mordeshoor her work—"

"Please," cried another Whichwoodian woman, "we'll do whatever you ask—just don't hurt us—"

"You will reinstate the mordeshoor to her former glory!" cried Baba gleefully. "You will treat her with reverence and respect—"

"We swear!" the Elders cried. "We swear on all that is dear to us!"

"And if you lie," said Baba in a low, lethal voice Laylee had never heard before, "we will come back for you."

The corpses roared and stomped their feet, unleashing animal-like howls into the night.

"Anything—*anything* you say—"

"Mordeshoor," said Baba, peering up at her in the night sky.

"Yes, Baba?"

"Do you accept the apologies of these monsters?"

Laylee couldn't help but smile. It was funny to see the weird wax remnant of her father refer to the perfectly normal humans as monsters. "I do, Baba *joon*."

"And if you need anything, you will call upon us to help you, will you not?"

"Of course, Baba," she said softly. "Thank you."

"And you're sure," said Maman now, "that you wish us to leave?"

Laylee nodded. "Thank you—thank you for everything. I'm not sure what I would've done without your help."

"You are never alone, sweet girl," said Roksana. "A kindness is never forgotten. Not even by those of us buried underground."

And Laylee watched the scene splinter apart from high in the sky, the spiderweb glittering behind her as a soft snowfall melted along its threads. Her dead friends and family quietly receded, tens of thousands of bodies marching peacefully through the streets, leaving the living Whichwoodians shaken in their wake.

Laylee, meanwhile, had never felt so happy or so powerful in all her life—and not because of the Elders who fell on their knees before her—but because her parents, she realized, had finally proven they loved her.

A nightingale sat upon Laylee's shoulder just then and sang her a song of congratulations.

"Thank you," Laylee said to the small bird. "Life is strange, isn't it?"

The bird nodded. "Yes," it said to her. "Things are seldom what they seem."

I DO
DEARLY LOVE
A HAPPY
ENDING

True to their word, the town never doubted her again.

Weeks passed, and things improved every day for our mordeshoor. Laylee was treated like royalty as she walked through town—faces no longer disgusted by the sight of her, but awed by the power they knew her to wield. The people were both terrified and impressed, and began offering her ungodly amounts of gold and silver to wash their loved ones. Talking to Laylee was soon considered a privilege—even being looked at by the mordeshoor was thought of as a gift—and Laylee, who did not care for the obsequious attentions of strangers, found great comfort in the company of her friends.

Ah, yes—her friends. They were still with her, of course.

Laylee had enough money now that she was able to hire the extra help she'd always wanted. And who better than the three people she trusted the most? Alice and Oliver and Benyamin were soon official employees of the mordeshoor, working decent hours alongside her during the day, and spending their evenings and weekends having . . . what was that word?

Fun.

Laylee tried attending public school again, but it was too difficult to be taught by teachers who were terrified of her and to sit beside students who wanted nothing but to hear her ghastly work stories. Eventually, Laylee asked Madarjoon if she wouldn't mind hometeaching her and her friends for a few hours every day, and Madarjoon nearly burst into tears at the request. Only too happy to oblige, the five of them—Alice, Oliver, Laylee, Benyamin, and Madarjoon—soon became a cozy little family. Oliver, who'd never liked his home very much anyway, could think of nowhere else he wanted to be—but Alice, whose parents were anxiously awaiting her, would not be able to stay forever. She'd been in touch with her father to tell him all that had transpired, and he was so proud of her for making things right with Laylee that he allowed her to stay in Whichwood, working alongside the others, for a period of no longer than six months. This was the average length of time a child was away from home for a task, so Father felt it to be fair.

For now, however, Alice would not think about leaving; there was simply too much to enjoy.

Alice and Oliver were living in Laylee's castle now, and each night was a chance for games and good food and long conversations over piping-hot cups of tea. There was always a roaring fire in the hearth and beautiful lanterns lit across the house. Madarjoon taught them how to cook rich stews and colorful rice; Benyamin showed Alice how to properly eat a frosted rose; and Oliver—well, Oliver began to change. He could feel himself settling into place for the first time in his life, and the steadiness—the safety—of simply *belonging* began to slough off his thorny, sardonic edges. He became a gentle soul—and would grow up to be a deeply thoughtful young man—and he came to love the infamous mordeshoor even more every day.

For now, however, they were the best of friends.

And tonight the living room was warm and bright and festooned with winter flowers. The snow fell softly outside the frosted windows of the old castle, and Laylee closed her eyes, humming along to a song she half remembered. Madarjoon was reminding Oliver how to set a table, while Benyamin and Alice carried steaming dishes into the dining room in preparation for their dinner. The air was thick with the aroma of saffron and fresh turmeric, cinnamon and salted olive oil; fresh bread was cooling on the kitchen counter beside large plates of fluffy rice, sautéed raisins, heaps of barberries, and sliced almonds. Feta cheese was stacked beside a small mountain of fresh walnuts—still soft and damp—and handfuls of basil, mint, scallions, and radishes. There were spiced green beans, ears of grilled corn, dense soups, bowls of olives, and tricolored salads. There was so much food, in fact, I simply cannot describe it all. But dinners like these were fast becoming tradition for the mordeshoor and her adopted family, and they would spend the evenings eating until their teeth grew tired of chewing, happily collapsing into sleepy heaps on the living room floor. There, they would finish out the night laughing and talking—and though they could not have known what the future would bring, they did know this:

In one another they'd found spaces to call home, and they would never be apart again.

❖

Until next time, dear reader.

THE END